IN THE MIDDLE OF THE END

Praxis's atmosphere had become superheated and un-breathable. From the high ground above the caverns, Rick glanced back at the wrinkled terrain. Volcanic light blasted through a dense shroud that stretched from the hills all the way to the base of a distant escarpment. And out of this storm two lone Veritechs flew, returning from a final reconnaissance patrol. Rick's worst fears were soon confirmed: not a safe region on the planet.

Beneath a swirling, agitated pall of cloud cover, Praxis was fractured beyond recognition. Great, furious rivers of molten stuff soursed across its surface, burying for-ests and villages in liquid fire. Praxis bellowed and roared like a tortured animal, rattling the GMU with its clamorous cries; the planet seemed to be expanding, bursting its geological seams, while Rick watched.

THE SENTINELS™ #3

DEATH DANCE

Jack McKinney

A Del Rey Book

BALLANTINE BOOKS • NEW YORK

FOR BEN WILSON,
WHO HAS HIS OWN ROLE
TO PLAY IN THE FUTURE.

A Del Rey Book
Published by Ballantine Books

Library of Congress Catalog Card Number: 87-91845

ISBN 0-345-35302-1

Manufactured in the United States of America

First Edition: June 1988
Sixth Printing: October 1990

Cover Art by David Schleinkofer

ROBOTECH CHRONOLOGY

1999   Alien spacecraft known as SDF-1 crashlands on Earth through an opening in hyperspace, effectively ending almost a decade of Global Civil War.

           In another part of the Galaxy, Zor is killed during a Flower of Life seeding attempt.

2002   Destruction of Mars Base Sara.

2009   On the SDF-1's launch day, the Zentraedi (after a ten-year search for the fortress) appear and lay waste to Macross Island. The SDF-1 makes an accidental jump to Pluto.

2009–11   The SDF-1 battles its way back to Earth.

2011–12   The SDF-1 spends almost half a year on Earth, is ordered to leave, and defeats Dolza's armada, which has laid waste to much of the planet.

2012–14   A two-year period of reconstruction begins.

2012   The Robotech Masters lose confidence in the ability of their giant warriors to recapture the SDF-1, and begin a mass pilgrimage through interstellar space to Earth.

2013   Dana Sterling is born.

2014   Destruction of the SDFs 1 and 2 and Khyron's battlecruiser.

2014–20   The SDF-3 is built and launched. Rick Hunter turns 29 in 2020; Dana turns 7.

Subsequent events covering the Tiresian campaign are recounted in the Sentinels series. A complete Robochronology will appear in the fifth and final volume.

CHAPTER
ONE

It was as if the Expeditionary mission was fated to strike a truce with someone, and the Regent just happened to be the only enemy in residence. In another five years the Robotech Masters would arrive in Earthspace, followed three years later by the Regis and her half of the Invid horde; but in 2026 (Earth-relative) this was still speculation, and for a few brief days there was talk of peace, trust, and other impossibilities.

Ahmed Rashona, *That Pass in the Night: The SDF-3 and the Mission to Tirol*

A FLEET OF INVID WARSHIPS EMERGED FROM THEIR transtemporal journey through hyperspace into the cool radiance of Fantoma's primary, like so many shells left revealed on a black sand beach by a receding tide. The mollusklike carriers positioned themselves a respectful distance from the moon they had captured then lost; only the fleet's mullet-shaped flagship continued its approach, menacing in its sealed silence.

At the edge of the ringed giant's shadow, Tirol's guardian, the SDF-3, swung round to face off with the Regent's vessel, the crimson lobes of its main gun brilliantly outlined in starlight.

Aboard the Earth fortress, in the ship's Tactical Information Center, Major General T. R. Edwards watched as a transport shuttle emerged from the tip of one of the flagship's armored tentacles. Edwards trusted that the Regent was aboard the small craft, accompanied certainly by a retinue of guards and scientists. The presence of the Invid fleet made it clear that any acts of aggression or duplicity would spell mutual annihilation for Invid and Humans alike.

Admiral Forsythe, who commanded the SDF-3's bridge in the wake of Lisa Hayes's departure with the Sentinels, was now in constant communication with the Invid flagship. It was the Regent who had taken the initiative in suggesting this extraordinary visit, but Forsythe had insisted that the fortress remain at high alert status at least until the Regent was aboard. Disillusioned by decades of war and betrayal, and hardened by the grim realities of recent reversals, it was the Human race that had grown wary of summits, distrustful of those who would sue for peace.

Scanners and camera remotes monitored the approach of the Regent's shuttlecraft and relayed relevant data to screens in the fortress's cavernous Tactical Center, where techs and staff officers were keeping a close watch on the situation. Edwards moved to the railing of the command balcony for an overview of the room's enormous horizontal situation screen. Studying the positions of the Invid troop carriers in relation to the SDF-3, it occurred to him how easy it would be to fire at them right now, perhaps take half of them out along with the Regent himself before the Invid retaliated. And even then there was a good chance the fortress would survive the return fire, which was bound to be confused. Numerous though they might be, the Invid seemed to lack any real knowledge of strategy. Edwards was convinced that their successful strike against the SDF-3 almost six months ago had been the result of surprise and old-fashioned blind luck. More to the point, he felt that he had an intuitive understanding of this enemy— a second sense birthed during his brief exposure to the brainlike device his own Ghost Squadron had captured on Tirol.

Edwards reminded himself of the several good reasons for exercising restraint. Apart from the fact that the actual size of the Invid fleet remained unknown, there was this Regis being to wonder about; her whereabouts and motivations had yet to be determined. Besides, he sensed that the Regent had something more than peace negotiations in mind. In any case, the data Edwards had furnished the Invid regarding the Sentinels' ship had already linked the two of them in a separate peace. But Edwards was willing to play out the charade—even if it amounted to nothing more than an opportunity to appraise his potential partner.

He dismissed his musings abruptly and returned to the balcony console, where he received an update on the shuttlecraft's ETA in the fortress docking bay. Then, giving a final moment of attention to the room's numerous screens and displays, he hurried out, adjusting his alloy faceplate as one would a hat, and tugging his dress blues into shape.

The docking bay had been transformed into a kind of parade grounds for the occasion, with everyone present as decked out as they had been at the Hunters' wedding extravaganza. There had been no advance notice of what, if any, protocols were to be observed, but a brass band was on hand nonetheless. The impression the Plenipotentiary Council wished to convey was that of a highly-organized group, strong and decisive, but warlike only as a last resort. The twelve members of the council had a viewstand all to themselves at the edge of a broad magenta circle, concentric to the shuttle's touchdown zone. A majority of the council had ruled against the show of force Edwards had pushed for, but as a concession, he had been allowed to crowd the bay with rank after rank of spit-shined mecha —Battloids, Logans, Hovertanks, Excaliburs, Spartans, and the like.

The shuttle docked while Edwards was making his way to a preassigned place near the council's raised platform; since he had been the council's spokesperson in arranging the talks, it had been decided that he represent them now in the introductory proceedings. Edwards had of course both seen and fought against the enemy's troops, and he had met face-to-face with the scientists Obsim and Tesla; but neither of these examples had prepared him for his first sight of the Invid Regent, nor had the Royal Hall's communicator sphere given him any sense of the XT's size. Like the lesser beings of the Invid race, the Regent was something of an evolutionary pastiche—a greenish slug-headed bipedal creature whose ontogeny and native habitat was impossible to imagine—but he stood a good twenty feet high and was crowned by an organic cowl or hood, adorned, so it seemed, with a median ridge of eyeball-like tubercles. Dr. Lang had talked about *self-generated transformations and reshapings* that had little to do with evolution as it had come to be accepted (and *expected*!) on Earth. But all the Protoculture pataphysics in the galaxy couldn't keep Edwards from gaping.

A dozen armed and armored troopers preceded the Regent down the shuttle ramp (a ribbed saucer similar in design to the troop carriers), and split into two ranks, genuflecting on either side of what would be the Regent's carpeted path toward the council platform. Recovered, Edwards stepped forward to greet the alien in Tiresian, then repeated the words in English. The Invid threw back the folds of his cerulean robes, revealing four-fingered hands, and glared down at him.

"I learned your language—*yesterday*," the Regent announced in a voice that carried its own echo. "I find your concepts most . . . amusing."

Edwards looked up into the Regent's black eyes and offered a grin. "And rest assured we'll do our best to keep you amused, Your Highness." He was pleased to see the alien's bulbous snout sensors begin to pulsate.

Edwards's one-eyed gaze held the Regent's own for an instant, and that was all he needed to realize that something was wrong—that this being was *not* the one he had spoken to via the communications sphere. But he kept this to himself, falling aside theatrically to usher the Regent forward to the council platform.

The Plenipotentiary members introduced themselves one by one, and after further formalities the Regent and his retinue were directed to the amphitheater that had been designated for the talks. The Regent's size had necessitated a specific route, along which Edwards had made certain to place as many varieties of mecha as he could muster. Each hold the summit principals passed through found combat-ready Veritechs and Alphas; each corridor turn, another squad of RDF troops or a contingent of towering Destroids. While aboard, the Regent's every word and step would be monitored by the extensive security system Edwards had made operational as part of his Code Pyramid project—a system that had also managed to find its way into the council's public and private chambers, and into many of the fortress's Robotechnological labs and inner sanctums.

There was a smorgasbord of food and drink awaiting everyone in the amphitheater's antechambers; the Regent nourished himself on applelike fruits his servants brought forth. Edwards noticed that Lang was doing his best to attach himself to the Invid leader, but the Regent seemed unimpressed, refusing to discuss any of the topics the Earth scientist broached. In fact, only Minmei succeeded in getting a rise out of the Regent. Edwards noted that the Invid could barely take his eyes off the singer after she had completed her songs, and he retained a slightly spellbound look long after the introductory addresses had commenced.

Terms for a truce were slated for follow-up discussions, so civilians and members of the press were permitted to enter the amphitheater itself. Edwards saw to it that Minmei was seated beside him in the front row, where the Regent could get a good look at the two of them.

The alien's initial remarks put to rest any doubts that may have lingered in Edwards's mind concerning the ongoing impersonation. The Regent spoke of misunderstandings on both sides, of a desire to bring peace and order to a section of the galaxy that had known nonstop warfare for centuries. He claimed to understand now just what had prompted the Human forces to undertake their desperate journey, and he sympathized with their present plight, hinting that it might be possible to accelerate the timetable for the Human's return trip to their homeworld—providing, of course, that certain terms could be agreed upon.

"It's a pity there has been so much loss of life," the Invid continued in the same imperious tone, "both in Tirolspace and during the so-called 'liberation' of Karbarra.

But while we may have no cause for further quarrel with your forces here, it must be understood that no leniency could be expected for those of your number who chose to join the Sentinels. And despite what you may have been told by the Tiresians, those worlds—Praxis, Garuda, and the rest—belong to me. The reasons for this are complex and at present irrelevant to the nature of these negotiations, but again we wish to stress that the Sentinels' cause was a misguided one from the start. It was inevitable that they fail sooner or later."

A charged silence fell over the auditorium, and Edwards had to restrain himself from laughing. The Sentinels had not been heard from for four months now. Official word had it that the *Farrago* was maintaining radio silence for strategic reasons. Then, recently, there had been open speculation that the ship had been badly damaged during the battle for Praxis. But Edwards knew better. He felt Minmei's trembling grasp on his upper arm. Colonel Adams, also seated in the front row, leaned forward to throw him a knowing look.

"We have only recently lost contact with the *Farrago*," Professor Lang was saying. "But I'm certain that once communications are re-established and an accord of some sort is enacted, Admiral Hunter and the others will abide by its terms and return to Tirol."

The Invid crossed his massive arms. "Yes, I'm sure they would have honored it, Dr. Lang. But I'm afraid it's too late. Four months ago the Sentinels' ship was destroyed—with all hands aboard."

A collective gasp rose from the crowd, and Edwards heard Minmei begin to sob. "Rick . . . Jonathan," she said, struggling to her feet, only to collapse across Edwards's lap.

Someone nearby screamed. Lang and the rest of the council were standing, their words swallowed up in the noise of dozens of separate conversations. News personnel and members of the general staff were rushing from the room. Edwards snapped an order to his aide to summon a doctor. Adams, meanwhile, was shoving onlookers aside.

Edwards held Minmei protectively. Once again he sought out the Invid's lustrous eyes; and in that glance a pact was affirmed.

But on Praxis the dead walked—those Sentinels who had escaped the destruction of the *Farrago*, and, unknown to them, a deadly host of archaic creatures returned to life in the bowels of the planet's abandoned Genesis Pits . . .

"Take a look for yourself," Vince Grant suggested, stepping back from the scanner's monitor screen. Rick Hunter and Jonathan Wolff leaned in to regard the image centered there: an intact drive module that had been blown clear of the ship and had fallen into low orbit around Praxis. Vince was reasonably certain the module's Protoculture-peat engines were undamaged.

"And there's no way to call it down?" Rick asked. "A hundred miles or so and an Alpha could reach the thing." Normally, one could fly a Veritech to the moon and back, but not one of the Sentinels' all-but-depleted Alphas was capable of attaining escape velocity.

Vince shook his head, his brown face grim. "We barely have enough power to keep the nets alive."

"Then it might as well be a million miles away," Wolff thought to add.

Vince switched off the screen and the three men sat down to steaming mugs of tea one of the Praxians had brewed up from some indigenous grass. After four months it had come down to this: the GMU's stores were nearly empty and foraging had become one of the group's primary activities. And in all those months they had yet to come up with an explanation for the disappearance of the planet's native population. What was left of the central city and all the surrounding villages were deserted. But whether what Bela called "the Praxian Sisterhood" had *chosen* to leave had not been ascertained.

Puzzling, too, were the tectonic anomalies and quakes that were continuing to plague the planet, as often as three times a day now. The quakes had convinced the Sentinels' Praxian contingent that Arla-Non—Bela's "mother" and the leader of the Sisterhood—had struck a deal with the Invid to move the planet's population to some other world. Rick wasn't sure if he bought the explanation, but it certainly served a therapeutic need if nothing else.

"Look," Rick said, breaking the silence, "they're probably already searching for us. Lang's not about to write us off. And even if the mining operation is *close* to on-schedule, they'll have at least one ship readied with the capability for a local jump. We just have to hope the Invid have lost interest in this place."

The horde's absence these months bordered on the conspicuous; and with the quakes and deserted villages, Cabell had speculated that it was possible the Invid knew something the Sentinels didn't.

Rick's optimism in the face of all this had Vince smiling to himself. *Rick would always be a commander whether he liked it or not.* "It's not Lang we're worried about," he said, speaking for himself and Wolff.

Rick caught his meaning. "Edwards has to answer to the council." There was an edge to his voice he didn't mean to put there. Lang had warned Rick about Edwards during one of the last links the *Farrago* had had with Base Tirol, and it was difficult to keep the memory of that brief deep-space commo from surfacing.

"Don't underestimate the man's ambitions, Rick," Wolff cautioned. "I'm sure they're going to come looking, but I'm willing to bet that Edwards will have the council eating out of his hand by then. Maybe one of us should have—"

"I don't want to go over old ground," Rick cut him off. "The only thing that interests me right now is a way to reach that drive module."

Grant and Wolff exchanged looks and studied their cups of tea. Rick was right, of course: there was no use dwelling on the choices they had made, individually and collectively. Wolff liked to think that at least Vince had Jean by his side and the precious GMU under his feet. But Rick had all but resigned his commission, and Wolff himself had left his heart behind.

A rumbling sound broke the silence, causing the mugs

to skitter across the tabletop. The tremor built in intensity, rattling the command center's consoles and screens, then subsided, rolling away beneath them like contained thunder.

No one spoke for a moment. Wolff wore a wary look as he loosened his grip on the edge of the table and sat back to exhale a whistle. "Course, Praxis could do us in long before the Invid or Edwards."

"Pleasant thought," Vince told him.

Rick gave them both an angry look. "We're going to get to that module if we have to pole-vault there."

Tactical concerns (and personal preference) had kept Vince Grant and Rick somewhat anchored to the GMU (which had been moved inland from its original seaside landing zone); but the rest of the substantially reduced Robotech contingent, along with the XT Sentinels, had opted for Praxis's wooded valleys, the planet's often glorious skies, and rolling hills. Max and Miriya's Skull Squadron had spent most of the past months reconning remote areas, hoping to come upon some trace of the vanished Sisterhood; but they had only succeeded in further depleting already critical reserves of Protoculture fuel. Consequently, the Wolff Pack stuck close to base, Hovertanks shut down. Bela and Gnea and the other Praxians had voluntarily detailed themselves to serve the group's logistical needs, and were assisted in this by the bearlike Karbarrans and vulpine Garudans. Cabell had all but isolated himself, disappearing for long walks from which he would return with samples of native rock or flora. Still a bit uncomfortable with the Humans and not yet fully accepted by the XTs, the Tiresian was often found in the company of Rem, Baldan, Teal, and the limbless Haydonites, Veidt and Sarna. Janice, too, had become an unofficial member of Cabell's eldritch clique, much to Rick and Lisa's puzzlement.

Presently, Cabell and Janice were off together on a long walk; they were on a forested slope about fifteen miles from the mobile base when the tremor that had shaken the GMU struck. The minor quake did little more than knock them off balance and loosen some gravel and shale from nearby heights; but it was the morning's second shakeup and it brought a severe look to Cabell's face.

Janice had thought to take hold of the old man's arm and utter a short panicked sound as the ground began to tremble. It was a performance worthy of Minmei's best, although Janice could hardly appreciate it as such—any more than she could fully understand just what had compelled her to seek out Rem and Cabell's company in the first place. That this should somehow *please* Dr. Lang was a thought as baffling to her as it was discomforting.

"There, there, child," Cabell was saying, patting her hand. "It will be over in a moment."

They recommenced their climb when the tremor passed. Janice disengaged herself and urged Cabell to go on with what they had been discussing.

"Ah, yes," he said, running a hand over his bald pate, "the trees."

Janice listened like a student eager for *A*'s.

"As you can see, they're nothing like the scrub growth we found on Karbarra—far healthier, much closer to the unmutated form." He motioned with his hand and went up on tiptoes to touch the spherical "canopy" of a healthy-looking specimen. The tendrils that encased the solid-looking sphere and rigid near-translucent trunk seemed to pulse with life. Gingerly, Cabell plucked one of the verdigris-colored applelike fruits, burnished it against his robe, and began to turn it about in his wrinkled hand.

"Even the fruit they bear is different in color and texture—although still a far cry from the true Opteran species. Nevertheless, it may tell us something." He took off his rucksack and placed the sample inside. "Look for the ripest ones," the instructed Janice, as she added a second fruit to the pack.

Cabell was straightening up when a sudden movement further up the slope caught his eye. Janice heard him start, and turned to follow his narrowed gaze.

"What was it?"

Cabell stroked his beard. "I thought I saw someone up ahead."

"A Praxian?" Janice asked, craning her neck and sharpening her vision.

"No," he said, shaking his head. "I would swear it was *Burak*!"

Later, a stone's throw from the grounded GMU, inside the wooden structure that had been designated both quarters and cell, Tesla wolfed down the fruits Burak had picked from the sinister orchard Zor's Flower of Life seedings had spawned on Praxis.

"Yes, yes, different, ummm," the Invid was saying in a voice tinged with rapture.

The young Perytonian tried to avert his eyes, but in the end couldn't help himself from watching Tesla as he ingested fruit after fruit. Moist sucking noises filled the cell.

"And you think they may have seen you?" Tesla asked him.

"It is possible—Cabell, in any case."

Tesla scoffed, still munching and handling the fruits as if they were wealth itself. "Cabell is too old to reconize the nose on his own face. Besides, they know I can't subsist on what you call food."

Burak said nothing. It was true enough: the Invid's food stock had been destroyed with the *Farrago*, and the Sentinels had agreed to place Burak in charge of securing alternative nutrient plants. But Cabell, who was anything but a doddering old man, and perhaps fearing the very transformations Tesla was beginning to undergo, had suggested that the Invid's fruit and Flower intake be regulated—this in spite of the fact that Tesla had to some extent ingratiated himself with the group since their victory on Karbarra. Each evening, Cabell and Jean Grant would look in on Tesla. Burak had been asked to furnish them with a daily log of the amounts gathered and ingested; and the devilish-looking Perytonian was complying—inasmuch as he would file a report. But the report was hardly a reflection of the actual amounts Tesla consumed. Fortunately, though, the Invid's transformations had been limited to brief periods following his meals, when neither Cabell nor Jean were present.

"More," Tesla said now, holding out his hands.

Burak regarded the Invid's newly-acquired fifth digit and pulled the basket out of reach. "I think you've had enough for today." Burak had heard it said that extraordinary powers could be gained from ingesting the fruits of Haydon's Worlds, but he had never understood that to mean physical transfiguration, and the Invid's recent changes were beginning to fill him with fear.

Tesla's eyes glowed red as he came to his feet, taller by inches than he had stood on Karbarra. "You *dare* to say this to me after all we've been through? You, who sought me out before fate landed us in this despicable situation? And what of your homeworld and the curse you were so feverish to see ended—have you given up hope? Would you renounce your destiny?"

Burak took a hesitant step toward the door, the basket clasped to him. "You're changing!" he said, pointing to Tesla's hands. "They're going to notice it, and what then? They'll cut back on the amounts, put someone else in charge of you. Then what becomes of your promises— what becomes of Peryton?"

Tesla continued to glare at him a moment more, transmogrifying even as Burak watched. The Invid's skull rippled and expanded, as though being forced to conform to some novel interior design. Gradually, however, Tesla reassumed his natural state and collapsed back into his seat, spent, subdued, and apologetic.

"You're right, Burak. We must take care to keep our partnership a carefully-guarded secret." His black, ophidian eyes fixed on Burak. "And have no fear for your tortured world. When the time comes for me to assume my rightful place in these events, I shall reward you for these efforts."

"That's all that I ask," Burak told him.

The two XTs fell silent as a gentle tremor shook the building.

Tesla stared at the floor. "I sense something about this planet," he announced, his sensor organs twitching as his snout came up. "And I think I am beginning to see just what the Regis was doing here."

CHAPTER
TWO

Unfortunately, there are no detailed descriptions of the Genesis Pits, other than Rand's colorful but highly personalized and impressionistic accounts (specious, as some would add), and the notes Colonel Adams hastily scribbled to himself while on Optera. And despite a plethora of theories and explanations, the sad truth is that the mechanism of the Pits remains a complete mystery— except to say that they were devices utilized by the Regis for purposes of creative evolution. Praxis apparently played host to the largest of these, and Lang, to name one, has speculated that the Pits not only gave rise to extinct creatures, but succeeded in regressing the entire planet to a formative stage of destructive vulcanism.

Zeus Bellow, *The Road to Reflex Point*

IF BURAK AND TESLA HAD BECOME THE SENTINELS' SIlent partnership, then Jack Baker and Karen Penn were certainly the group's inseparable pair. But that, each liked to believe, was merely a result of duty assignments. And even four months on Praxis hadn't provided them with enough time to work through the competitive trifles that fueled their relationship. They were not only marooned, but marooned together; and Praxis had become the proverbial town that just wasn't big enough for the two of them. Bela, Praxis's wasp-waisted local sheriff, was only one of the contributing factors; but Karen nevertheless took every opportunity to keep Jack as far from Bela as she could, often encouraging the Hovercycle recons that had become something of Jack's stock-in-trade.

A joyride disguised as a scouting mission had brought Jack and Karen to a series of caves two hours out from the GMU. Lron and Kami had ridden with them. Four months had given the Sentinels plenty of time to grieve for those who had gone down with the *Farrago*; but Karen often wondered just how long it was going to take for her to grow accustomed to her XT comrades. She wasn't a bit xenophobic—a fact that had won her a place with the Sentinels to begin with—and in actuality it wasn't so much the strangeness of Lron or Kami that overwhelmed her, but the *similarities*. If only Karbarrans didn't so resemble Kodiak bears, she would tell herself. And if only Kami didn't look like upright versions of the foxes she used to see near the cabin her father had once owned . . . She had much less trouble with Baldan and Teal, with their bodies of living crystal. Or Tesla, for that matter—now *there* was an alien you could *believe* in!

But wolves and bears and snail-headed things . . . Karen was in the midst of wishing that Bela had had a more alien form—even a more *rotund* form—when without warning, Jack hissed: "Cut it out!"

The four Sentinels were well into the central cave now, inside a huge vaulted corridor that was as hot as blazes and reeking of sulphur. Curiosity had drawn them in; but Jack, never one to do things halfway, had insisted they go "just a little further," and here they were a good half a click along. There were primitive sketches on the walls of the caverns they had passed through—depictions of hideous spiderlike creatures Jack claimed were "symbols"—and Karen was in no mood for fun house games or laugh-in-the-dark surprises.

"Huh?" she said, gulping and finding her voice.

"I said cut it out."

"I know what you said, Jack . . ."

She threw him an angry look in the darkness, wondering suddenly if she had actually *voiced* some of her private musings about Bela. Then all at once something hit her on the top of the head. XTs or not, she decided, someone was trying to be funny. Karen whirled around, hoping to catch Kami in the act, but he was way off to her left inspecting a chunk of rock near the cave wall. Lron, too, seemed to be preoccupied with other things. So, wiping sweat from her face, she turned back to Jack, and said, "Not funny."

"What?"

She put a hand up to shield her eyes from his miner's light. "Throwing things. I'm not real thrilled about being in here to start with."

"I didn't throw anything," he started to say, when Lron's gurgling snarl interrupted him.

"Who hit me?" the Karbarran growled.

Jack felt a tap on his shoulder, swung to it, then instinctively looked up. His light illuminated what looked like an assemblage of globular-shaped deposits on the cave's ceiling. Suddenly he saw one of the things move, and realized that it was some sort of free-floating, translucent sphere. Kami switched on the light strapped above his muzzlemask and shined it on another portion of the ceiling; here were more spheres, ranging from baseball size to almost four feet in diameter, all bobbing against the rock like helium balloons.

"What the . . . ?" Jack said, moving his head around, the beam finding more and more globes. "Jeez, the place is crawling with them."

"Jack!" Kami shouted, training his light on something further along the corridor. Everyone turned in time to see a medium-sized globe emerge like a bubble from a conelike projection in the cave floor. Jack rushed ahead, watching the milky thing ascend, and soon found himself perched on the rim of a large shaft, roughly circular and belching up a lot of heat and noxious fumes. Kami, Lron, and Karen joined him a moment later, just as another globe was beginning to make its way up and out.

"What a stink," Karen commented.

Warily, Jack reached out to touch the basketball-sized orb. It was hot, but not dangerously so; what surprised him was the thing's misleading solidity.

"Jack, don't," Karen warned him when he tried to capture it.

But as was so often the case with Jack, the warning came too late: no sooner had he taken hold of the sphere than it shot toward the ceiling, lifting Jack off the floor.

Arms extended over his head, he rode it up for fifteen feet before letting go and landing on the other side of the cavern in a neat tuck-and-roll that blew out the miner's light.

"Yeah!" he whooped, as Kami helped him to his feet. It wasn't unlike the spill he had taken six months ago in Tiresia, but this time he had landed among friends.

Karen hauled off and whacked him in the arm. "Jack, can't you just—"

"That thing took off like a rocket! Almost pulled my arms out of the sockets."

"Yeah, we noticed, Jack," Karen said, miffed.

They were all staring at the ceiling now.

Jack watched the spheres bob against one another. "Almost seems like they're looking for a way out of here, doesn't it?"

"Yeah, just like we are," Karen and Lron said at the same time.

In the commo chamber of his hivelike domain on Optera, the Invid Regent received a transmission from the simulagent who was representing him on Tirol. It seemed that the so-called *Humans* now occupying the Robotech Masters' ravaged and forlorn moon had put on quite a show—with the kind of pomp and circumstance the Regent strived to imitate. He was almost sorry he hadn't gone there himself. What with most of his remaining fleet anchored in Fantomaspace, was there really anything to fear? he asked himself. Still, the fact remained that there were too many unanswered questions. What, after all, did the would-be commander of the Human forces—this Major General Edwards—want? He had been so quick to come to the Regent's aid in that matter of the Sentinels' ship . . . But it bothered the Regent that the Human had yet to ask for anything in return. Did he simply wish to capitalize on the Sentinels' defeat to move himself higher in the chain of command, or were these machinations part of some larger scheme?

In a certain sense the answer was unimportant, the Regent decided at last—providing he could make use of that factionalism that divided the Human forces.

He regarded the image in the communications sphere, catching a look in his double's eyes that troubled him. "Is there news of Tesla?"

"There is," the simulagent said. "It appears the Tesla was aboard the *Farrago* when our forces destroyed it."

Tesla, dead, the Regent thought. It touched him in a way he would never have believed possible. But perhaps it was not true, perhaps there were survivors of that battle? He had yet to hear from the follow-up forces who had been sent in to resecure the planet. "Who seems to be in charge?" he asked after a moment.

"As you surmised," the simulagent continued, "there are signs of an ongoing power struggle, principally between Edwards and a certain Dr. Lang—a scientist who did his best to charm me during the introductory sessions."

"Is Lang the weaker one, then?"

"No . . . no, this is not my belief. The scientist in fact seems to have the backing of the Humans' council—an assembly that functions as a kind of governing body."

The Regent found the idea odd—as he had the puzzling gerontocracy the Robotech Masters had favored. He couldn't understand how *twelve* minds could agree on anything, when he and his queen—merely *two* minds—had quarreled over every decision.

"Then, you must work on Edwards," the Regent said. "Promise your continued support in his petty struggle if it comes down to that. Tell him we'll join forces. But just make certain you learn the whereabouts of their homeworld and how they came to possess Protoculture. It may be that they know more than we do about Zor's matrix or the Masters' destination."

"Am I to make no demands of Edwards in return for our support, Your Highness? It hardly seems a wise move."

The Regent stared at the sphere's image in disbelief. Was this some evil mirror he was looking into now? "Just what would you have me demand?" he asked, seething under the restraint he kept in his voice.

"The brain, to begin with. Along with their promise to keep out of the sectors we still control."

The Regent made a dismissive motion toward the sphere. "These things are obvious, servant. What else is on your mind?"

"Minmei," the simulagent said without explanation.

The Regent made an irritated sound and scowled. "What's a Minmei?"

"The Human female that sang for my benefit."

The Regent caught himself from staggering back from the sphere. He had only the vaguest understanding of this thing called singing, but the implication was clear enough: the simulagent was flawed in the same way that the Regis was. She had allowed herself to be seduced by Zor, and now this pathetic creature the Regent had sent to Tirol was falling victim to the same perverse urge! *Was there no end to these injustices!*

"Hear me, grub," the Regent growled, hood puffed up like a poisonous sac. "My reach is long enough to end your life where you stand. Do my bidding, or feel the power of my wrath."

The simulagent genuflected for the remote eye of the sphere. "My lord."

"Now and always," the Regent said, shutting down the device.

Rick had spent the better part of the Praxian day inside the GMU, brainstorming with Vince and Wolff about possible ways to contact the orbiting Spherisian drive module. Onboard computers had calculated the period of the module's eccentric course, and gone on to project just how much Sekiton fuel the thing contained, how far the module could be expected to fold, and just when its newly-attained orbit around Praxis might decay. But there were still no solutions to the big questions of how to reach the module or bring it down.

Rick left the base just before sunset, as had become his habit this past month, and joined the core group in their makeshift camp on the outskirts of the Praxian inland city.

He wasn't fond of the scene, which reminded him more of a recreational campground than the billet it was supposed to be. Things were not just lax, but *loose*, as though everyone but him had grown to accept the situation. There was a logic to it, of course; it made no sense to walk around tied up in knots. But just the same, Rick had no patience with complacency, and he silently hoped that an idea would come to them one night while sitting around these campfires comparing cultural notes. So he stood in line with the rest of them now, Human and XT alike, and helped himself to the Praxian gruel the mess staff was cooking up to supplement the reconstituted meals and nutrient pills taken from the base's dwindling stores. Moreover, these sessions were the only waking hours he got to spend with Lisa—the *new* Lisa, that was, the liberated Lisa.

Where Gnea and Bela were still unforgiving of Miriya Sterling's Zentraedi past, they had embraced Lisa as though she were a long-lost member of the Sisterhood. At first Rick was not entirely unhappy about it, but all at once Lisa seemed a different person than the one who had argued so strongly against his joining the Sentinels to begin with. And while it was true that what was good for Lisa was good for the group, Rick couldn't help but feel a bit, well, *jealous* of the partnership Gnea and Lisa had formed. The Praxian seemed to draw this sort of reaction everywhere she stepped. Rick knew that Karen was having troubles with her, and he guessed that even Bela must be harboring some ambivalent feelings about her friend's sudden preoccupation with Lisa.

With Gnea it was martial skills that mattered most; but beyond speed and strength, Lisa had discovered something else: an independence and self-assertiveness that was taking some getting used to.

Rick had these thoughts in mind when she came over to sit beside him in the firelight, still flushed and exhilarated from her latest weapons training session. She talked about the *feel* of the halberd in her hands, the power of the *naginata*; she was practically poetic in describing Gnea's crossbow and two-handed shortsword. Rick took it all in, forcing a smile and offering all he could in the way of appropriate nods and utterances; but behind the smile his mind was doing backflips. *What next?* he asked himself. Would he come out here one evening to find her parading around in some skimpy fighting costume, like Bela's bossed and D-ringed body harness? Would she suddenly take to buccaneer boots, some totem-crested helm, long-bladed dirks and throwing knives? Rick shuddered at the thought, grateful for the fact that that damned Robosteed, Halidarre, was temporarily grounded. Unfortunately, however, the Praxian's lambent-eyed malthi, Hagane, was not, and the winged pest nearly parted Rick's hair as it came darting in just now to settle itself on Bela's bulky forearm sheath.

Rick muttered a curse and looked over at his wife. "Glad to hear how well it's going," he told her. "And I'm sure all this'll come in handy at the next Tirol decathlon."

She looked at him askance and took a forkful of food from his plate. "Something bothering you, Rick?"

"No, no, I mean, it's good to see you keeping busy, Lisa."

"Is that what you think I'm doing—'keeping busy'?"

Rick inclined his head, eyes narrowed. "It's what we're all doing, isn't it? What am I supposed to do: spit in my palm and pledge my fealty to someone? 'For the Eternal She and the glory of Haydon!'" Rick mimicked.

"Rick—"

"No, really. Maybe we should all be practicing sword-play and crossbow technique, leaps and high jumps. Then maybe one of us'll be able to reach that module instead of wasting away down here."

Almost everyone in the circle caught an earful of Rick's words, and the usual evening's chatter abruptly ceased. The fires crackled, and four Hovercycles could be heard approaching the perimeter. Lisa and Rick seemed to be locked in an eye-to-eye contest when Jack, Karen, Kami, and Lron entered the camp. Jack took a long look around, oblivious to the uncomfortable silence his swaggering entrance had dispersed, and announced cheerfully: "Wait'll you hear what we found."

"They've agreed to help us," Veidt said later on, hovering into the cavern where Rick and some of the other Sentinels were puzzling over the hideous cave paintings Karen had pointed out. "If 'agreed' is the proper word."

Karen noted that there were fewer globes than there had been that afternoon; several had apparently found their way out, as evidenced by the fact that one or two had been found bobbing against the ceiling close to the mouth of the cave.

"Then they are life-forms?" Rick said.

"Oh, most assuredly."

Rick heard Bela snort behind him. After Jack had told them of the find, the Praxian women claimed to have heard tales of these orb creatures from Arla-Non, chief of the Sisterhood. But the things were believed to be extinct, just as the beasts depicted on the cave wall were—or so Rick and the others hoped.

They had all tried to convince Rick that the orbs could wait until the morning, but he had insisted Jack lead them back to the caves immediately. Now, not quite four hours since Jack's return to the base, Rick and half a dozen or so of the core group were standing in the floodlit heat of the cave, listening to the results of Veidt's telepathic probe.

"I register no sense of how they came to arrive here," the mouthless Haydonite was mind-speaking, motioning to the cavern. "I only know that their destiny lies somewhere in space. This condition of . . . *levity* is but a transitional stage in their life cycle. They are sentient, in what might be termed a primitive, or instinctual, fashion. But the important thing is that they seem to understand our need for their assistance—their *support*, if I may be permitted to play with your language some. In fact, Sarna and I detect a certain desperateness to their own flight—as if they are not merely obeying a behavioral directive, but are, in quite a real sense, escaping."

No one felt a need to state the obvious: Praxis was a

tectonic nightmare from which they all wished to awaken. The heat and stench of the cave only reinforced that fact. And if the cave was indeed a volcanic vent of some sort, it was no wonder the globes were anxious to leave.

Cabell, his face and glabrous pate beaded with sweat, was watching one of the smaller creatures now, as it bobbed its way toward the entrance. He couldn't help but be reminded of Tiresia's antigrav spheres, and he began to question if there wasn't some mysterious connection here.

Rick was watching the same sphere; but he was wondering just how many it might take to lift an Alpha to the edge of the Praxian envelope. "Do they understand what we're asking of them?—the specifics, I mean."

Veidt hovered over to a position directly beneath a cluster of the creatures.

"The mecha should lift off on its own power," Sarna answered for him. "After that, Veidt and I will be able to herd the orbs into place."

Excited, Rick punched the palm of his hand. He swung around to Jack and Karen. "Contact the GMU. Tell Vince to round up the Skull and the Wolff Pack. We've got to work fast and assemble a crew for the module."

"Will we be heading back to base?" Karen thought to ask.

Rick shook his head. "Give Vince our position. Tell him what we've learned." He glanced up at the globes, rivulets of sweat running down into his eyes. "I want the base to come to us."

While members of the Sentinels hurried to break down the camp and ready the GMU for motion, Burak was breaking the news to Tesla. The Invid made him repeat it several times until satisfied he had all the details straight.

He had felt certain all along that he wasn't fated to end his days on Praxis, and now Burak had brought word that Hunter and the others had discovered a way to reach the orbiting drive module. With precious little time to spare, Tesla thought as he and Burak packed away the few belongings the Invid kept in his cell.

Ever since his earlier ingestion of the mutated fruits, his mind had been reeling, locked in a kind of revelatory state, where answers came to him full-blown, like short-lived explosions of light. He had been asking himself why the Regis had come to Praxis in the first place; it was a question that had been plaguing him on and off for months now.

It was before the mutiny aboard the *Farrago* that they had encountered one another, when Tesla had landed on Praxis to choose specimens for the Regent's zoo. The Regis had given him a vague explanation then, and it didn't occur to him until much later on to question her responses. With the continual quakes to spur him on, however, and the aid of the fruits, the answer became obvious: she had come here to conduct further Genesis Pit experiments—part of her grand scheme to transmute the Invid race into something Tesla himself could not yet begin to imagine. Optera had been the site of the first Pits, where Tesla and most of the other evolved Invid were birthed. But the Regis's experiment there had almost doomed the planet; it had, in fact, touched off the initial search for secondary worlds she might employ. Abandoning Optera and the Regent, she had finally come to Praxis to hollow out new Pits deep in the planetary core. And of course that was why she had left the place—because her experiment was following the same course it had taken on Optera.

Left. But for *where*? Tesla asked himself . . .

He put a hand on Burak's shoulder as they were about to leave the room. "You say they will be choosing a crew to pilot the first Alpha up to the module?"

Burak felt the strength of the Invid's grip, and tried to shake it off, but could not. "Are we going to die here, Tesla?" he asked in a faltering voice. "Peryton, my people—"

"Quiet, you fool!" Tesla stepped through the doorway, glancing around to assure himself that no one was within earshot, then swinging back around to Burak. "We won't die here—not if we're part of that crew, we won't."

Burak's face contorted. "But how—"

"You leave that to me. I just need to know one thing."

Tesla sniffed at him. "Can you pilot that Spherisian module?"

"I suppose so," Burak said uncertainly.

Tesla stretched out his thick neck. "Then we're all set."

In Admiral [Rick] Hunter's personal notes [recorded on Praxis], we learn of several discussions that took place between Cabell and Bela regarding the issue of child-bearing among the Praxians. (Hunter himself was nonplussed to hear Bela refer to Arla-Non as her "mother.") [Bela] even allowed Cabell to tour the whaashi—"birthing center," or creche—although refused to enter it herself. It was understood that certain members of the Sisterhood were preselected to receive female "offspring," who were then raised as "daughters of the Sun." The Praxians had little understanding of courtship, sexuality, or pregnancy; the "coupling rite" being a kind of catch-all mystery that was at the same time enticing and fearsome. Cabell, of course, was quick to see Haydon's hand at work.

A. Jow, *The Historical Haydon*

OF ALL THE WORLDS SHE HAD VISITED, THIS WAS THE saddest, the Regis decided as she contemplated Haydon IV's cityscape from the uppermost tier of the Invid headquarters there. It was a small world, perfect in every respect, but with a heart as lifeless as the faceless beings who hovered across its surface and seemed to know one's every thought. The Regent liked to believe that he had conquered the place by cajoling his way into a position of absolute authority; but Haydon IV had seen many a would-be ruler come and go, while it itself remained unchanged, ungovernable, unreachable. It was one of the few open trading ports left since the Tirol-Optera war had spread like some contagion through the Quadrant; and as such Haydon IV enjoyed a semblance of peace. Still, the Regis sensed the presence of an incomprehensible evil here, far worse than the vulcanistic horrors her Genesis Pit experiments had unearthed on poor Praxis.

She had come to see for herself what the Invid scientists had found here, and now, as grateful as she was for the data they had supplied her, she could feel nothing but a kind of vague dread for the future, for the very path she had embarked on. Haydon IV's sophisticated scanners had picked up a trace of the Robotech Masters' course, and in effect pointed a way to Zor's ship with its matrixed Flowers. But the Regis's private samplings of the planet's vast store of metaphysical knowledge had revealed something of potentially greater import—a suggestion that she had been as self-deceived as the Regent had been. That her ostensibly *evolved* nature—along with her continuing efforts to search out the physical form deemed most perfect to embody her intellect—was but a carefully constructed delusion, self-generated and engineered to keep her from the real truth. And yet it was a truth she refused to contemplate, a mating she would not accept—one she was not at any rate *prepared* to accept.

There would come a moment years hence when these truths would dawn on her like the primordial fireball itself, and the Invid Regis would willingly surrender the shackles of physicality and ascend; but just now, she chose to keep Haydon IV's revelations from her thoughts, and turn her attention to the Praxian woman who had requested audience.

"This world is a paradise," the Regis said, turning from the spire's incomparable view, but gesturing to it nevertheless. "I have traveled the Quadrant over, and never have I known such an exquisite place."

Arla-Non flashed her a scornful look, and tossed back a luxuriant mane of sun-bleached hair. "Better a cave on Praxis than a palace here," she sneered. "Every nerve in my body screams at me to beware this place, this planet. Every breath of its wind carries a lie."

She was tall and powerfully built, clothed in swaths of colorful fabric and knee-high boots of soft hide. Looking at her, the Regis couldn't help but be reminded of her own failed attempts to emulate that racial form, to please Zor . . .

"Is that fair?" the Invid Queen-Mother asked, an edge to her voice as she approached the Praxian. "You knew nothing but hardship, and now you have luxury beyond the dreams of most beings."

"And you have Praxis," Arla-Non shot back.

The Regis made an impatient gesture. "You must learn to forget Praxis, as *I* have Optera. Your world is doomed."

"So you continue to tell me. It is your way of decreeing that Praxis had become nothing more than an Invid breeding ground."

"Praxis will breed nothing but asteroids!" the Regis seethed. "I cannot change the past, Praxian. Make your peace with this world, or live out your days in torment. I offer you no other choice."

Without a word, Arla-Non spun on her heel and headed for the entrance to the spire's transport shaft; she stopped short of its triangular accessway. "I can choose to fight you to the last, Invid."

The Regis had her back turned, but the Praxian's words found their mark. She was beginning to understand why the Regent had never regarded persuasion as a viable option where force could be employed. The Regis made note of it, promising death for the next beings who attempted to thwart her.

Praxis, meanwhile, was beginning to come apart.

Forced by ground swells, fissures, and rock slides into taking the long way around, the GMU arrived at the caves precious hours behind its projected ETA. But with the region's numerous caves and shafts to vent the planet's internal pressure, the land here had been spared some of the tectonic turmoil afflicting other areas. Nevertheless, the air was filled with static charge, heat, and stench, and the cave that housed the orbs was fast becoming unworkable. The Skull had arrived hours earlier, and by the time Vince and Jean Grant, Janice, Rem, Wolff, Burak, and the others stepped from the mobile base, the rest of the core Sentinels were well into Rick's impromptu briefing. Several dozen orbs of varying size had already exited the cave, and were well on the way to their enigmatic deepspace destiny; but Veidt and Sarna had "persuaded" the stragglers to lag behind awhile longer. Kami and Learna had reported the emergence of yet more spheres from the cavern's internal chimney. Cabell speculated that it might be possible to widen the access some, and thereby increase the chances of additional creatures reaching the surface.

The plan called for the spheres to lift an Alpha with a crew of five clear through Praxis's suddenly albescent atmosphere. Once in space and under its own power, the mecha would complete the rendezvous with the drive module. When that was accomplished, the crew would drop the module into a lower orbit while the spheres continued to raise five-person crews. It was conceivable that the GMU would have to be abandoned, but at least the VTs and Hovertanks would survive. Although it sounded crazy the plan was straightforward enough; there remained, however, several variables to deal with. First, the Sentinels had no idea how many orbs might be required to lift a VT, or just how fast they would be able to raise it the requisite distance. An incorrect guess could leave the mecha hanging in space waiting for the module to complete another orbit, or, worse still, missing the thing altogether. Second, and equally problematic, the initial crew would have to be comprised of personnel capable of piloting the module into a lower orbit, and possibly—should the orbs for some reason withdraw their *support*—through a spacefold to Karbarra, or equidistant Fantoma. Third, someone was going to have to stay in touch with the orbs.

This last issue had been decided by the time the GMU contingent joined the others near the cave entrance. Sarna was going to be in charge of mustering and instructing the creatures in their task. Veidt had simply said, "Sarna will do it," and no one argued the point. Rick now had the module in mind.

Most of the XT aliens were out of the running for this slot, except Veidt—who was needed down below to mindlink with the spheres—and Lron. Rick had doubts that the burly Karbarran could successfully pilot the ship through a jump; and although the module was Spherisian in design, neither Teal nor Baldan were qualified to handle it. Vince was needed for the GMU. That left only Lisa, unless . . .

"Janice," Rick said suddenly, "can you handle it?"

Burak almost volunteered, but Tesla restrained him at the last moment, gesturing him silent while everyone's attention was focused on Minmei's former partner.

She nodded, without saying anything. If it came down to a fold for Tirol, Lang would be delighted to find her aboard. She sensed Lisa looking at her, and gave her a tight-lipped but understanding look.

"Lisa?" Rick said, figuring he would be safer with a crowd around him.

"I'm fine with your choice, Commander," she told him evenly. "But just who do you have in mind to pilot the Alpha?"

Rick looked around uncomfortably. "Well, I think I'm the most qual—"

Half-a-dozen voices interrupted him at once.

"It's too risky," Max said, speaking for all of them. "I'll go."

"Your place is with the Skull," Rick pointed out firmly, and everyone grumbled their agreement. Several of Max's squadron volunteered, including Miriya, but Rick rejected all of them for one reason or another. Then Jonathan Wolff stepped forward.

"I'm the logical choice," he said, addressing the circle. "With Vince and Max, we'll still have our air-and ground-based forces intact in the event of a follow-up attack. One less tanker isn't going to influence things one way or another."

Rick had to smile at Wolff's attempt at humility; but Wolff's reasoning was sound. "All right," he said at last, "you've got it."

Just then Tesla began to shoulder his way to the center of the circle. "Commander, I, too, would like to volunteer my services." He turned to the Sentinels, some of whom were already ridiculing him.

"You've all seen how I can be *made* to cooperate. But

now I wish nothing more than to demonstrate my *willingness* to cooperate. These four months have taught me a great deal about freedom and self-determination, and I would urge you all to begin to accept me as a member of your group, rather than a prisoner. Should the Regent's troops appear in Praxis-space, I will be there to foil them, much as I did in Tracialle."

Rick looked up at the Invid, remembering what Lisa had told him of the *Farrago*'s attack on the Karbarran city, and wondering whether Tesla was genuine or simply trying to save his own green skin. Rick asked him if he wasn't growing tired of his role—whether he had any reservations about betraying the Invid cause.

"It seems to be my lot in life," Tesla said in a theatrical manner. "Besides, I want this mission to succeed as much as the rest of you do."

Rick exhaled a short laugh. "We appreciate that, Tesla. But intentions aside, I think you might be too . . . uh, *large* for the mecha."

"Too large!" Telsa said as though insulted. "Put me in the Beta's cargo section, then." He sucked in his breath, as if to narrow his bulk, and waited, making an effort to *will* the right words into the Human's mind.

"You think we can fit Burak and Tesla back there?" Rick asked Wolff hesitantly.

Wolff sized up the Invid and the horned Perytonian, who was looking a bit peaked. "Be a little tight, but I think we can manage them."

"Then let's hop to it," Rick said decisively.

Tesla and Burak lingered for a moment at the hub of the sudden activity. The Invid turned partway toward his accomplice and spoke in a hushed voice.

"Make certain you bring plenty of fruit aboard, my young friend. Destiny calls to us both."

On Tirol, too, things were off to a shaky start. During the first session of the truce negotiations, the Regent had thrown a kind of temper tantrum, which only Edwards recognized as being as false as the Invid himself. He had a perfect understanding of the imposter's aim, and so was hardly surprised to learn afterward that the XT had informed Dr. Lang and the council he would henceforth meet with Edwards only. The Regent had explained how difficult and *alien* it was for him to discuss terms with a *body* of representatives—especially when one of those twelve was a Zentraedi, with whom the Invid would never make peace. Once again Lang had tried to set himself up as ombudsman, and once again the Regent had rejected him out of hand. Edwards was the Human the Regent would talk to, and none other. Lang let the council know that he was against any one-to-one arrangements and insisted that his arguments be added to the record. But Edwards was delighted to hear that the council had overruled the scientist's objections and that Longchamps and the others were counting on him to see the talks through to their completion.

Just now the simulagent and the traitor were seated across from one another in Edwards's spacious quarters aboard the SDF-3. The two of them had already put on quite a show in the fortress amphitheater, but here they were safe from the prying eyes of the council and free to speak their minds. Edwards had decided to play it close to the bone, and congratulated the Invid on his performance.

"Why, whatever do you mean, General?" the false Regent said after a short silence.

There was just enough hesitation in the Invid's response to reassure Edwards that he was dealing with an imposter, but it benefited him to play along. "Your words for the council's scanners," Edwards told him. "All that talk about how there's more than enough room in the Quadrant for both our races."

"We are a reasonable people," the false Regent returned, sipping at the green grog he had brought with him.

"Yes, of course, you are. I'm encouraged by the very fact that you've come to Tirol. There are some who didn't believe you would."

"And you?"

"Oh, I think you're capable of almost anything, Your Highness."

The Invid set aside his goblet and looked across the desk at Edwards. "You speak boldly for one your size, Human. Are all those from your world so courageous?"

Edwards sat back in his chair and grinned. "To a man."

"And your weapons speak with equal power . . . But it intrigues me: how exactly did you come by your Protoculture systems?"

"We took them away from the Zentraedi," Edwards said, leaning forward on the desk. "They were annoying us."

The simulagent studied his four-fingered hands. "And you came here in search of their Masters?"

"We came here to finish the job, if you want the truth. Word had it that they were going to be showing up in our neighborhood, so we decided to take the fight to them instead. Save our planet the inconvenience of a backyard war."

"Yes, but you seemed to have missed them."

"We'll catch up." Edwards shrugged. "First we've got a little business here to take care of."

The Invid ignored the remark. "Just where is your 'neighborhood,' General?"

Edwards touched his faceplate. "A long way from Tirol."

"Yes, but where?"

"West of the Moon, east of the Sun."

"You trifle with me," the XT said menacingly.

Edwards shot to his feet and put both hands flat on the desk. "And you waste my time! What are you after?"

The Invid met his glare. "The return of the brain."

"In exchange for what?"

"Your lives," the Regent hissed.

Edwards laughed and walked away from the desk, only to whirl around and say, "You needed my help to eliminate a single Karbarran ship. And I know that your fleet is spread so thin you can hardly protect the worlds you've conquered. So what makes you think you can intimidate me now?"

The Regent, too, was on his feet, filling one half of the room. "I thought for a moment we were on the same side, General. But perhaps I was mistaken."

"You've already been more help to me than you know," Edwards told him. "But the brain stays until you've got something better to offer me than threats."

"Your egotism will be the death of you," the Regent said from the door.

Edwards smiled as the door slid shut. Everything he said had been calculated to draw out the real Regent; talk was useless until then. But he had faith that his gambit would pay off. Eventually the Regent would show himself —in person or as before in the sphere—and when that day came, there would be much to discuss.

Incredible as it seemed, the armored Alpha was actually being carried aloft by perhaps three dozen orbs of mixed size, clustered like grapes beneath the mecha's swept-back wings and Beta-elongated fuselage. Cheering seemed a bit premature, but that didn't stop any of the still-grounded Sentinels from sending up exclamations of encouragement.

The feat had required more orbs than anyone would have guessed—over a quarter of the number that remained in the cave, at last count—but Veidt, as promised, had been able to herd them under the hovering VT without much ado. Several of the creatures either didn't comprehend the Haydonite's telepathic instructions or thought better of them at the last moment and opted for solo flights into Praxis's cloudy and smoke-smudged skies. The others, however, rose quickly to the task, less like lighter-than-air balloons than anti-Galilean cannonballs. Cabell calculated that if the present rate of lift remained unchanged, the mecha would arrive at the Roche limit with ample time to rendezvous with the drive module. At that point, Sarna, copiloting the Alpha along with Jonathan Wolff, would bid the orbs what amounted to a "thanks and so long," and the VT would utilize its onboard computer and thrusters for guidance adjustments. Janice, Burak, and Tesla were squeezed together in the mecha's Beta hindquarters.

Rick threw a couple of enthusiastic shouts to the Alpha before rushing off to join Vince and some of the others, who were already in the GMU's command center monitoring the mecha's progress and supplying its telemetry systems with updates gleaned from the base's scanners and data mainframes.

Wolff was on the net when Rick entered the command center. "Everything checks out fine so far," he was telling Vince. "It's like an elevator ride to the stars." The net was relatively clear, except for occasional bursts of static.

"Ask him if Sarna anticipates any disengagement problems," Rick said to Vince.

"Uh, no problem," Wolff reported a moment later.

Rick leaned in to one of the console pickups. "And Janice?"

"Here, Rick. We're doing all right." Thumping noises could be heard in the background. "It's just a little close for comfort."

Rick made a mental note to tell Janice just how much he admired her. "Sit tight, Janice. You're almost there."

Wolff and Janice acknowledged and signed off. Rick found himself crossing his fingers, something he hadn't done in years. He laughed in a self-mocking way, optimistic but oddly disturbed at the same time.

Outside the base, members of the Skull Squadron and the Wolff Pack were beginning to prepare a second mecha for lift. This one was to include Lisa, Miriya, Cabell, Lron, and Crysta. The air was filled with lightning flashes and all-but-constant peals of thunder. Praxis trembled underfoot like the SDF-3 during fold maneuvers. Even Cabell refused to speculate on how much time the planet had, but to a few of the Sentinels each minute felt like something to be thankful for.

Kami and Learna had yet to emerge from the orb cavern deep inside the region's now-floodlit central cave. The temperature had dropped considerably over the past half hour, and the air was breathable once more. Baldan and

Teal had joined the Garudans to help keep count of the orbs, and with the first Alpha on its way, Jack, Karen, Rem, and Gnea appeared on the scene.

Everyone watched as two golf ball-sized spheres wafted up out of the shaft to join their brethren, who were grouped in various locations along the vaulted ceiling. A veritable parade of overhead orbs stretched from here all the way to the mouth of the cave. Jack directed his light down into the shaft and asked Karen and Gnea to do the same. He had discerned some sort of movement perhaps eight feet down the well; one of the larger creatures was struggling to fit through the constricted passageway. Each time the thing would back off, two or three smaller orbs would bubble up and out of the shaft. The Sentinels had discussed various ways to enlarge the opening, but Rick was leery of employing explosives or lasers for fear the orbs would misunderstand their intentions. Jack couldn't, however, see any harm in spelunking down for a closer look.

While Gnea and Rem went rushing back to the GMU for cord and anything they could find in the way of rigs and harnesses, Baldan and Teal were off in a corner of the cavern exploring a different route down. It had occurred to the male Spherisian—earlier, when he had melded his hand with the cave wall—that there were peculiar forces at work in the depths of Praxis, and Teal, her arms buried to the elbow in rock, was affirming that now.

"The mineral content is most unusual," she reported analytically. "Nothing like what we've experienced elsewhere on Praxis. It seems more a part of the planet's past than its present."

"I sensed the same thing," Baldan told her, gesturing to the cavern's outcroppings and formations. "These deposits have been exhumed from somewhere in the core, but in some unnatural fashion. They're not so much the result of the planet's vulcanism as they are the *cause* of it." Once again, Baldan pushed his arms deep into the wall. "Perhaps I can travel the Crystal Highways here as we do on

Spheris, and communicate with the tortured substrata of this world."

"It's dangerous," Teal said, pulling one of Baldan's hands from the wall. "Praxis is destabilized. You might not be able to re-form . . ."

Baldan registered surprise at her concern for his well-being; it was unlike her. "Then keep hold of my hand," he said as he began to meld the rest of his crystalline being with the glistening rock that formed the cave wall. Teal could see a portion of the wall assume Baldan's features in bas-relief; he seemed to smile, then disappeared entirely.

"Good luck," she whispered, still grasping her friend's disembodied hand.

Elsewhere in the cavern, Rem, Gnea, and Karen heard Jack say, "There are thousands of globes down here! Enough to lift the whole damn base!" His voice rose from the shaft like that of an oracle. "They're huge ones! We've gotta give them a way out! Tell Hunter—"

Just then a violent tremor hit the cave, erasing Jack's words and eliciting a shower of rocks and dirt from the grotto's ceiling. The orbs began an excited dance when the tremor passed, hastening toward the entrance in what seemed an inverted ball-bearing stampede. Karen was leaning into the shaft yelling Jack's name.

"I'm okay," he yelled back at last. "Just took a spill off the rope. I'm on a ledge or something. Seems to be some kind of cavities down here . . . One of you better come down—and bring more light."

Teal had been knocked to her knees by the force of the quake, but she had managed to keep hold of Baldan's hand and forearm. She twisted around in time to see Kami and Learna picking themselves up off the floor. Then she saw Baldan's face manifest in the wall: he looked terrified.

"What? What is it, Baldan?"

His stone mouth formed the word *Invid*. "They've performed a horrible experiment here, brought back creatures from the planet's past—like these globes, but terrible ones also. You must hurry and warn the others. These creatures—"

"But you can't expect me to leave you here!" Teal was aghast.

"I'm trapped," he told her. "It's no use."

Teal tugged on his arm. "Don't—" Then she looked down and noticed a fissure in the wall that hadn't been there before the tremor.

"Baldan . . ."

"Hurry," he insisted.

Reluctantly, she let go of his arm. And as she turned to leave, she heard Karen scream from across the grotto.

"It's Jack and Rem!" a wide-eyed Karen was saying when Teal approached her. Kami, Learna, and Gnea were trying to calm her. "Something's taken hold of them!"

FOUR

*[The psychohistorian] Constance Wildman would have us be-
lieve that the Robotech Wars were nothing more than a series of
incestuous struggles and Freudian-inspired rivalries—the Masters
and their "children," the Zentraedi; the various intrigues that
blossomed around "primal goddess" Lynn-Minmei; the Flower as
grail, nutrient mother's milk . . . And she adduces the Regis-Tesla-
Regent triangle to strengthen her case; for where else "do we find
a more perfect archetypal representation of the rebellious son who
wishes to kill the father and possess the mother?" To which one
might be tempted to answer: in the relationship between Zor and
Haydon.*

> Footnote in Reedy Kahhn's *Riders on the Storm: The Re-
> gent's Invid*

"**A**ND YOU ACTUALLY THREATENED EDWARDS?"
the Regent's voice screamed through the communicator.
"You fool! You were supposed to entice him, not drive him
further from my grasp."

In his quarters on the fleet flagship, the Invid simulagent gulped and found his voice. "I was only trying to get
information out of him—as you yourself requested. But he
wouldn't reveal anything about his homeworld. And worse
still, he didn't seem to believe me when I spoke of the
power of our empire."

The Regent made a sour expression. "Well, how could
he, coming from the likes of you? Do you know nothing of
subtlety? Have you forgotten all that the brain taught you
about intelligence gathering? It's as though you've made
up your mind to deal with the Humans in your own sloppy
fashion, when your mission was to be my eyes and ears.
Not my mouth!"

The simulagent winced, and turned to see if any of the soldiers were laughing behind his back. How could he begin to explain what he was going through—how the *feel* of power had worked its own magic on his mind, a magic that outweighed any concerns for diplomacy or "subtlety." But he kept these things tucked away from the being he was born to answer to, and instead thought to address the Regent as one might expect a servant to behave.

"I apologize, Your Highness. It's these Humans . . . they confuse me."

"Yes," the Regent told him, softening his tone some, "I can understand that much. But I begin to wonder about this Edwards. It strikes me that perhaps he has seen through my ruse—no thanks to you."

The simulagent lowered his snout to the communicator remote. "Tell me how I can make amends. I am but your humble servant."

The Regent wagged a finger. "And it would profit you to keep that in mind." He showed the sphere the palms of his hands. "*Why* does everyone feel they can think for themselves? First my wife, now you . . . Only Tesla served me well." He waved his hands in the air. "*Arg*, this whole affair is my fault anyway, sending a servant to do a conqueror's work." The Regent adjusted his robes. "I want you to return to Optera. There's nothing more you can do on Tirol, and if I permit you to stay any longer, it's likely you'll *undo* something."

"But, Your High—"

"Don't argue with me! We can do without the captured brain a while longer, and there are other ways to extract the information we want about the Masters, the Matrix, and the Humans' homeworld. Better to let the situation on Tirol deteriorate of its own accord. Then Edwards and I will talk." The Regent's eyes stared out from the sphere, gazing coldly at his simulagent. "You may have my looks"—he sighed—"but you certainly lack my talents."

Rick slammed his hand down on the console-mike stud and shouted Wolff's call sign into the pickup. One minute

Jonathan had been reporting that all signals were go for disengagement, and the next thing anyone knew he was saying something about the Beta having separated from the VT. And now the GMU seemed to have lost contact with both components.

"Rising Star, come in," Rick urged. "Wolff! Respond. What's going on up there?" He swung around to Jean and Vince, who were busy at adjacent consoles. "Anything?"

Jean swiveled to face him. "Too much cloud cover for a visual on the Beta, but scanners show it on an accelerated course for the drive module. The Alpha's way off the mark. We should have some data soon."

"Was it the globes?"

"Can't tell, Rick," Vince said without turning around.

Just then Wolff's voice crackled into life through the room's speakers. "—actly sure what happened. Sarna was just passing along instructions to the orbs, then all of a sudden the Beta broke away. We're way off course. Can you give us a new heading?"

"Coming up," Rick answered him. "Do you have any traffic from Janice?"

"Negative, Rick. I can't even get a fix on the ship."

"She's closing on the module, Jonathan," Vince said. "Any guesses?"

"Not right now."

Rick was about to add something when the hatch hissed open. "We've got troubles, sir," a Skull pilot announced.

"We're aware of it," Rick said, more harshly than was necessary.

The captain took a puzzled look around. "No, sir, in the caves. We're under attack."

"Attack? From what?" Rick noticed for the first time that the woman was covered with dirt. Her face was smeared with some unidentifiable black fluid or grease.

"Uh," the pilot stammered, "you're going to have to decide for yourself, sir."

Rick and the pilot left the base at a run. Outside, Rick saw scores of orbs streaming from the mouth of the cave. Veidt and a handful of Praxians and mecha pilots were doing their best to calm the creatures, but Max and Miriya, along with half the Wolff Pack, were nowhere in sight.

"In here, sir!" the pilot was shouting, motioning to the cavernous entrance.

The floor of the cave was shaking, and Rick heard low rumbling sounds he initially attributed to tectonic tremors; then he realized that he was hearing explosions. These grew more concussive as he neared the grotto.

The place was in a state of near pandemonium, dozens of orbs bobbing along, underlit by intense flashes of explosive light that was pouring out from holes and shafts in the floor; strident voices raised above the clatter of weapon fire; and something else—a kind of shrill, clacking noise, as eerie as it was loud.

Rick glanced around, trying to make sense of things. Karen Penn was off in a corner, terrified, although Kami and Learna were by her side. Teal stood some distance from them, alone near what looked to be a limb of rock. Gnea and Bela were carrying coiled lengths of cord toward a shaft opening; close by were a couple of Perytonians and a few men from Wolff's team, donning gas masks and strapping on web-gear ammo packs.

Without warning someone thrust a Wolverine into his hands.

"Max!" Rick said, whirling around. "What's—"

"Cover up," Max cut him off. He tossed Rick a mask and trotted off toward the shaft, cradling an Owens Mark IX mob gun. "Jack and Rem are trapped down there," he called over his shoulder. "We've killed a bunch of them already, but they just keep coming!"

"Killed a bunch of what? Who keeps coming?"

At the opening, Max pulled down his respirator and hooked on to one of the cords that had been lowered into the shaft. "Ready?" he shouted above the din from down below. Breathless, Rick followed his lead, and the two of them took to the rigs.

A moment later, on the floor of an enormous sublevel room, Rick was certain they had overshot their mark and landed in hell. In the strobing light he could see they were standing on the rim of a massive well that seemed to drop straight down to the planet's molten core. Here, too, the ceiling was covered with orbs—most of them of greater size than any he had seen on the surface; but it was the creatures crawling up out of that well that had left him speechless. They might have been Hovertank-size spiders, except for their eyestalks, double-tiered segmented bodies, and front-facing mouths. And if they weren't the devil's own creation, Rick decided, then he didn't ever want to meet their maker. For no god could have loved so hideous and evil-looking a beast.

It thrilled him to realize that the black stickiness coating the cavern's floor was blood from these things, but even that was not enough to wash the fear out of him. He remembered reading somewhere that there was an actual endogenous terror hormone certain creatures gave rise to in the human body; and indeed he seemed to *remember* them in some primal corner of his mind. But then he suddenly recalled where he had actually seen them: they were the creatures an ancient and unknown Praxian hand had depicted on the cave's walls!

Tesla was amazed by the Human female's strength. He had finally succeeded in dragging her backward into the Beta's cargo space and now had both of Janice's seemingly frail wrists firmly clasped in his own hands, but it had been a struggle all the way. Burak, meanwhile, had slid forward into the cockpit seat to handle the controls. The drive module was looming into view through the VT's canopy, right on schedule, and theirs for the taking.

"Welcome to our crew," Tesla was saying to the still-untamed female. "Glad to have you aboard." Jonathan Wolff's urgent voice could be heard over the open net.

Janice twisted around, almost breaking free of his hold, and glared at him. "Is this any way to treat a guest?"

"If I let you free, will you promise to behave?"

Janice gave her head a defiant toss. "Try me."

Tesla eased his grip, and the android everyone thought a woman lunged for Burak's neck. Tesla pinioned her arms and threw her roughly against the aft bulkhead; he was pleased to see some of the fight go out of her.

"Burak," Janice said weakly, one hand to her head. "What's your part in this? I can't believe you'd leave your friends to die back there."

Burak showed her his profile, velvety horns and heavily boned brows accented amber in the display lights. "It's the only way I can help free my planet," he offered. "You can't understand—"

"Enough of this," Tesla interrupted, taking stock of the wounds Janice's fingernails had opened on his arms. "Pay attention to what you're doing. And shut down the comm," he added, gesturing to the net switch.

The crystalline-shaped Spherisian module filled their view now, eclipsing the stars. Burak matched the Beta's course to the module's seemingly slow-motion end-over-end roll, and began to maneuver the mecha along the drive's scorched and much-abused hull. He utilized the on-board computer to communicate with the module's own, and within minutes the docking-bay hatch was opened; the Beta was home free.

When the bay had repressurized, the trio climbed from the Beta cockpit and eventually found their way to the bridge. Tesla carried Janice the entire way, bear-hugged to his huge chest like some sort of stuffed toy he couldn't live without. Burak lugged along the mutated fruits he had smuggled aboard the VT before liftoff.

The Invid was feeling omnipotent—not only because he had so easily outwitted the Sentinels, but because he would soon be on his way to Optera for the face-to-face encounter with the Regent he had so often envisioned these past periods. The fruits from Karbarra and Praxis had, so he believed, rendered him superior to the monarch he had once served as soldier and would-be son. And now it was time for the Regent to step aside and grant him his due position as leader of the Invid race. Tesla had come to understand that it took more than mere strength to lead; it took insight and vision, and these gifts were his in abundance.

But as they arrived at the drive's control room, some

very real problems presented themselves, eroding Tesla's
fantasies and summoning an anger from his depths.

"But you told me you could astrogate this ship!"

With a gesture of helplessness, Burak turned from the
starmaps and spacefold charts he had called up on the
Spherisian guidance monitors. "I thought I could, but
now . . ."

Tesla stormed over to him and began to scan the
screens, puzzling over the datascrolls. He pointed a thick
finger at one of them. "Here. Here is Optera."

Burak's eyes opened wide. "Optera! But, Tesla—Peryton, we're going to Peryton."

Telsa pushed him aside. "In due time," he said absently.
"First there is something I must attend to."

Burak steeled himself. "Then attend to it without my
help."

Tesla made a violent motion with his hands, but checked
himself short of the Perytonian's neck, taking him instead
by the shoulders, fraternally. "Of course, my dear. To Peryton, then." Tesla's hands urged Burak down into one of
the acceleration seats. "Now, why don't we try to figure
this out together, step by step. Let's just say for example's
sake that we *did* want to fold for Opteraspace . . . Now,
how would we do that, my friend . . . ?"

Janice took in the exchange from across the room. The
two mutineers had all but forgotten about her, so it was
easy enough to jack into the drive's systems while their
attention was focused elsewhere. In a short time she had
completed her bit of cybernetic magic. No matter what
they fed into the ship's astrogational computers now, the
module was locked on course for the Fantoma space system.

Janice smiled to herself, wondering how Tesla would
take to surprises.

At first it was believed that Baker and Rem had been
captured or eaten by the bristly eight-legged crawling
nightmares delivered up from the Praxian netherworld; but
subsequently the Sentinels found that their two teammates

were simply being *detained*—the word someone from the Wolff Pack had used. Jack and Rem had been probed and manhandled, but apparently were safe. It seemed that the arachnids—Gnea and Bela had a name for them no one could pronounce—had no taste for meat. Moreover, the creatures weren't on a feeding frenzy at all—nor, for that matter, were they interested in counterattacking the beings who were busy lancing them with lasers and rockets. Like the orbs, these living anachronisms—unseen on Praxis for millennia—were attempting to flee the storms that burned at the planet's transformed core.

Rick was long past his initial fright, but the sour taste of fear remained in his mouth. It struck him as odd that while in his day he had fought fifty-foot giants and walking slugs, ridden into battle alongside humanoid clones, ursine warriors, and amazons on Robotsteeds, he could experience such utter terror at the sight of giant spiders. Maybe, he had decided, it was the very mindlessness of the creatures; after all, even the Invid weren't *monsters*, were they? The Praxian women had been equally frightened, and Rick tried to imagine what it might be like to go up against, say, *dinosaurs*.

But if the creatures hadn't actually added to the Sentinels' plight, they had done nothing to improve things. Countless orbs had exited the cave, and now there was a nasty bit of mopping up to do down below while the rest of the orbs were mustered for further lift assists. To make matters worse, there was still no word from the Beta, and one of the Spherisians had gone and gotten himself *stuck in a rock*!

Presently, Rick and some of the others were grouped around Teal and the hand that had once belonged to her friend. Baldan was merged with the wall—the way a Mesoamerican bas-relief could be said to be merged to a stela. His profile was frozen but plainly visible, and there was a crystalline mass protruding from the section of rock where his chest might have been. The crystal grew before the astonished eyes of the assembled group.

"No, you can't, Baldan—please stop this!" Teal was

shouting to the wall. She swung around to Rick. "He is attempting to transfer his essence. But this has never been achieved on any world' but Spheris." She looked back at the engorged growth. "And I don't want to raise it!"

Again the crystal enlarged. Teal put her hands to her head in a panicked gesture and pleaded with Baldan to stop. But ultimately her hands reached for the faceted thing and she began to tug at it.

"It's no use, Baldan," she cried. "It will die!"

Rick moved in to give her a hand, and with some effort the two of them managed to pull the crystal loose. The hollow *pop!* sent a shudder up Rick's back. Baldan's profile receded into the wall and vanished. Teal dropped the crystal from her trembling hands and regarded it.

"The child is lifeless . . . dead." She looked around at the others. "Baldan is lost to us."

Whimpering sounds found their way out from under Kami and Learna's breathing tubes. Rick took Teal by the shoulders. "What did he tell you?"

She stared at him blankly for a moment, then said, "The Invid. They must have been using Praxis for experiments of some sort. It was the chambers they hollowed out that gave birth to those creatures. And these same chambers have ushered in this world's demise."

"But what kind of experiments?" Rick demanded. "What were they trying to create?"

Teal shook her head.

Tight-lipped, Rick released her and motioned a radioman over to him. "Any word from the Beta?" he asked Vince when the GMU link was established.

"They've reached the module," Vince updated. "But we're not getting through to them."

Rick summarized what had gone down in the caverns. "I want to speak with Tesla as soon as they call in. He must know something about all this—these *pits*. Maybe there's a way to reverse it?"

"Unlikely," Vince responded. "But I'm sure Tesla will tell us what he knows. He's practically one of us now."

* * *

With a little help from the GMU's computers, the Alpha was back on course. Wolff and his Haydonite copilot were at a loss to explain the unexpected separation, but they assumed Janice had done so with some good purpose in mind, and that her radio silence was nothing more than a glitch in the system. It didn't occur to either of them that there was conspiracy afoot.

Wolff continued in this hopeful vein, even after he had learned that the Beta had apparently made a successful docking with the drive module. That singed piece of orbiting space debris was above him now, and he was getting all he could from the Alpha to make up for lost time. It was only when his radio requests for docking coordinates were ignored that he began to suspect foul play. The hunch became full-fledged concern when he couldn't get the Alpha's onboard systems to interface with the module. Consequently, the docking-bay shields remained closed, and unless something could be done to open them, the Alpha was going to wind up dead in space.

Even if that meant going extravehicular.

Sarna took over the controls while Wolff suited up. Praxis turned below them like a cataracted eye. The telepath strapped in, bringing the Alpha as close as she could to the module's scarred hull; then Wolff blew the canopy. He floated up and out of the VT on a tether line, took hold of the side of the pinwheeling ship, and tried to center his attention on the alien external control panel. Sarna spoke to him through the helmet relays, avoiding the net in favor of frequencies of a cerebral sort. Wolff heard her thoughts as spoken words as he fumbled with Spherian switches designed for hands more sensitive than his own.

But a short while later the hatch was sliding open and pocketing itself in the crystalline hull. Sarna engaged the Alpha's attitude jets and began to maneuver the ship to safety.

The Beta was inside, empty; and fortunately, Wolff decided, there was no welcoming party there to greet them. Down on the hold floor now he armed himself with a rifle and two handguns; Sarna had perfect recall of the module's corridor and compartment layout, so she led the way. They were barely out of the docking area when the ship lurched.

"We're leaving orbit," Sarna told him.

Wolff felt the rumble of the module's drives ladder its way up his legs. Sarna hovered along the corridor at an increased pace, then abruptly right-angled herself into a large cabinspace and told Wolff strap himself into one of the seats.

Wolff regarded the acceleration couch and threw her a questioning look.

"We're preparing to fold," she told him.

"They've *what*!"

"They folded," Vince Grant repeated. "The module's gone."

Rick leaned against one of the GMU command-center consoles to catch his breath. He had run all the way from the cave only to hear the bad news as soon as he came through the hatch.

"But, but, did they—"

"Not one word," Jean cut in. "The last message we had was from Wolff. He was sure something had happened to Janice."

"Tesla," Rick said, biting out the name.

Vince nodded. "That's my guess."

"But where's the Alpha now?" Rick added, looking back and forth between the two of them.

Jean pushed herself back from the console, her hands on the arms of the chair. "That's the weird part. The Alpha made it aboard."

Rick fell silent; it felt for a moment as though they were speaking to him in a foreign tongue. He shook his head, hoping everything would settle into some sort of order. "Maybe it wasn't Tesla. Maybe Janice knows something we don't . . ."

"Okay," Vince said.

"And maybe she managed to get word to Wolff, but he couldn't reach us . . ."

"Okay, again."

"And maybe they *had* to fold because they realized there was no way to get everyone offworld using the VTs..."

"Uh huh." Vince folded his arms. "So they take off for Karbarra or Tirol, figuring we'll be able to wait it out."

Rick left it unanswered. There was no need, anyway, now that the tremors had recommenced. A steady, thunderous roar filtered into the room; somewhere nearby, mountain ranges were beginning to crumble.

It was a short jump. Wolff could feel himself coming out of the fold's dizzying effects, and was on his feet even before Sarna had furnished him with an all-clear sign.

When the two of them burst onto the module's bridge, they found Tesla and Burak seated at the controls. Janice was off to one side, asleep, Wolff thought.

Tesla and Burak both swung around as they heard the hiss of the hatch. The Invid's snout dropped open when he saw Wolff standing there armed to the teeth, and he immediately fell backward against his coconspirator, hoping Wolff would read it as Burak attempting a capture.

The two XTs rolled across one of the console benches and down onto the floor. Taken completely off guard, Burak didn't know what had hit him. But Tesla was forcing himself into a subordinate position now, and ordering Burak to grab him by the neck.

"Fight, you idiot!" Tesla was whispering. "You've go to make them believe you had nothing to do with this!"

Burak finally got the message and threw his hands around the Invid's thick neck. The two of them butted heads and snarled and cursed at each other. Burak was working his thumbs up Tesla's snout by the time Wolff succeeded in pulling him away.

"Back off!" Wolff told him, brandishing one of the handguns. "Tesla, on your feet!"

Sarna hovered over to the com.

The Invid raised his hands, but remained on his knees, pleading with Wolff not to kill him, and confessing to his attempt to seize the ship.

"And if it wasn't for this horned fiend I'd have—"

"Cut the crap," Wolff said. He turned around to Burak, who was trying his best to look innocent, even heroic. "You threw in with this slug."

"I didn't!" Burak argued. "He put a spell on us!"

"A spell?" Wolff almost laughed. "You mean he *made* you do it?"

Burak pointed to Janice. "Ask her if you don't believe me."

Janice had reactivated herself. She looked at Wolff and said, "They were in it together—"

"Liar!" Burak yelled.

"—but they couldn't seem to agree on a destination. So I made the decision for them."

Tesla and Burak traded looks.

"Where are we?" Wolff said, as confused as anyone else.

"Fantoma," Janice said, and Tesla fainted.

CHAPTER
FIVE

Betray (I looked it up): to deliver to an enemy by treachery or disloyalty; to be unfaithful in; to seduce and desert . . . Is this what I'm guilty of? Have I seduced and deserted him? Am I delivering Jonathan over to an enemy? Have I been unfaithful? As I repeat the word over and over to myself, it begins to lose all meaning; it becomes a meaningless sound, a bit of Tiresian or Praxian babble. But then I begin to think of it as a kind of war cry, a sound that echoes back and forth across the terrain of my life and these twenty years of bloodshed. If I am a betrayer, I am also the betrayed. I am the SDFs-1, 2, and 3; I am all the councils and all the generals. I am the dead, the War itself.

An excerpt from the journal of Lynn-Minmei

WITH RICK AND LISA AND ALL THE OTHER MEN and women who had joined the Sentinels' cause missing and presumed dead, there were precious few people Dr. Lang could trust, let alone seek out for company or old-fashioned good counsel. Things had not been the same between Lang and Harry Penn since Karen left, and of the Plenipotentiary members, only Justine Huxley and Niles Obstat were still receptive. Edwards had influenced the rest to one degree or another, except of course for Exedore, who had become Lang's unofficial ally and close friend. Even Lynn-Minmei had been turned—by what, Lang wouldn't even try to imagine. Lang, however, was well accustomed to isolation; so even when it wasn't self-imposed he could get by. He had been managing to hold his own with the council, in spite of Edwards, and at the same time was overseeing both the mining operations on Fantoma and the repairs to the SDF-3. But the Regent's visit had introduced something new and threatening to the horizon: the possibility of a partnership between Edwards and the Invid. Lang had seen Protoculture shape stranger events these past twenty years, but none so potentially dangerous—to the Expeditionary mission, to Tirol, to the Earth itself.

Something within him refused to accept Hunter's death; he knew he wasn't standing alone here, but he had nevertheless been powerless thus far in persuading the council to launch a rescue ship—even now when there were several available with the capability for the required spacefold, some running on Sekiton, some on the recently mined monopole fuels. But it was the Regent's behavior at the introductory summit sessions that finally convinced him to take matters into his own hands. And it was that decision that brought him to Fantoma. He had allowed his godson and apprentice, Scott Bernard, to accompany him, but left Exedore behind on the fortress to safeguard their mutual interests while the Regent's fleet remained anchored in Fantomaspace. The crew of the newly christened prototype dreadnought he had commandeered—the unnamed SDF-7 —was one that had been handpicked for the journey after a bit of chicanery by himself and General Reinhardt; they were a capable and loyal lot, commanded by Major John Carpenter, who was being considered as a candidate to head up the first return mission to Earth.

Lang's reasons for choosing Fantoma could be summed up in one word: *Breetai*. He was aware of the hostilities that had cropped up between Breetai and Edwards over the issue of the Regent's arrival, and he knew precisely where the Zentraedi's loyalties lay. And where Breetai went, so followed his hundred-strong cadre of sixty-foot biogenetically-engineered warriors—a force to be reckoned with no matter what the council's ultimate decisions might be.

No sooner did Lang step from the shuttle that had ferried his party to the surface of the ringed giant than Breetai insisted on escorting him through a tour of the mining complex. It was obvious that the Zentraedi was taking some pride in his accomplishments, so Lang didn't offer any resistance. But the opportunity to discuss the pressing issues that had brought him here didn't present itself until much later on, and by then Lang was nearly feverish. Breetai had led them to a massive Quonset-style structure that served as the colony's command and control center— the only such building in New Zarkopolis designed to accommodate both giants and Humans in relative comfort. There, Lang reviewed what had been said during the so-called truce talks, and what *reported* statements had been exchanged between Edwards and the Regent during the subsequent one-on-one sessions. Breetai said little, preferring instead to listen or grunt an occasional exclamation of anger or surprise. But when Lang finished—with an audible sigh—the Zentraedi collapsed his steepled fingers and leaned forward in his chair, gazing intently into the Humans' balcony area.

"One part of me wants to blame Admiral Hunter for allowing things to come to this," he told Lang. "But if anyone can appreciate the unpredictable nature of these things, I can." Lang didn't have to be reminded of the bizarre reversals the Zentraedi commander had witnessed and suffered through; and in this the scientist and warrior were brothers of a sort. "I suggest we take steps to secure our position against Edwards."

"Yes, but how?" Lang asked.

"Just as you have begun," Breetai said, motioning to where Carpenter and his exec were seated. "And you must arrange for additional mecha to be sent here . . ."

"Disguised as mining devices perhaps."

"Exactly. We have our own ship, our own mecha, but we must have our own weapons. New Zarkopolis could become our base of operation. And of course we possess something even more important than firepower . . ."

"The ore," Lang completed.

Breetai nodded. He had his mouth opened to say something more when a Human at the comm console interrupted him. "Report from the fortress," the tech announced, straining to hear the communique. "A ship has entered the system. Colonel Wolff and some of the Sentinels are said to be aboard."

"Thank God," Lang said, throwing his head back.

Breetai wore an enigmatic look. He touched his faceplate in an absent manner and rose from the chair to tower over the "Micronian" balcony.

"The Protoculture is at work again. We call out and it answers."

"Yes," Lang directed up to him. "And would that we could always predict its response."

Word of the drive module's approach spread to all stations and was relayed down to Tirol's surface. In her canteen in Tiresia, Minmei swooned upon receiving the news. She had returned to the surface only hours before, and now she tried to collect her thoughts before hastening back to the city's shuttle staging area.

At the same time in his quarters aboard the SDF-3, T. R. Edwards was in the midst of a session with the false Regent.

"It seems you were a bit premature in reporting the destruction of the *Farrago*," he said with a malevolent grin. Even the Invid's black, unreadable eyes failed to conceal a sense of shock; but the simulagent quickly rallied.

"And perhaps the data you supplied was in error," he countered angrily.

The Invid imposter had taken it upon himself to have one more go at winning Edwards over, despite the Regent's orders to the contrary. He had given careful thought to the Regent's harsh criticisms and was convinced that a followup discussion was in order. He now thought he had a clear understanding of the concept of sublety; but like Tesla he was not big on surprises, and the sudden appearance of the Spherisian module had completely undermined his efforts.

Edwards was waving a forefinger at him. "There, there, Your Highness, no call for insults, is there? Just when we were getting along so *famously*." Then Edwards's face grew serious, his one eye cold. "Besides, it's just a couple of our people and one of yours. There were bound to be survivors."

"One of mine?" the simulagent asked, alarmed.

"Tesla—isn't that his name? Or didn't you know he was aboard?"

The Invid curled one his sensors. "You failed to mention that."

Edwards shrugged. "What's the difference? He's alive." *And so is Wolff*, Edwards thought. He glanced across the desk at the Invid, beginning to tire of the game. Would this Tesla be able to confirm his suspicions? he wondered, making a note to have the returnees monitored at all times. "Now, what was it you were saying before?"

The simulagent tore himself from concerns about the possible consequences of encountering Tesla. "I—I was about to make you an offer, I think."

Edwards waited for him to continue, then laughed. "Well, go ahead—let's lay our cards on the table."

The simulagent held up a hand. "Three planets—yours for the choosing. Free access to all the other worlds I control—a limited partnership—and last, my help in realizing your, *dreams*, shall we say."

Edwards felt his jaw. "In exchange for the brain . . ."

"And Tesla . . ."

"And Tesla."

"And one thing more."

Edwards's brow went up.

"I want Minmei."

Wolff and company stepped out of the module and onto the deck of the SDF-3 docking bay to the sound of cheers —a few, at any rate, from a section led on by Emil Lang, Lord Exedore, and several staff officers. And it was Lang who clasped Wolff's hand and wrist, as if he had never been so happy to see someone. Behind him, Janice was getting the same treatment; Sarna, Burak, and Tesla were all but ignored.

"What the hell's going on?" Wolff asked the scientist straightaway. "You've got half the Invid fleet out there!"

"There's much to discuss," Lang shouted as press and officers jostled one another to get close. "But tell me—the others—Rick and Lisa—"

"They're alive," Wolff returned, buffeted about by the crowd. "But they won't be much longer if we don't get a rescue ship to Praxis."

Lang frowned. "Well, we have to see about that."

"What do you mean, 'see about that'?" Wolff gestured back to the module. "We didn't have enough fuel to jump back, but Praxis—"

"Things have changed," Lang told him, just loud enough to be heard. "We have to talk."

Wolff felt something acidic wash through him. All the while he had been answering Lang's questions, his eyes had been darting around the hold, searching for some sign of Minmei. Now, after seeing a hundred Invid ships anchored in Fantomaspace, and with Lang's portentous whisperings in his ear, he found her, and the sight only served to double his dread. She was standing alongside Edwards, among that unresponsive group, offering him a weak and pathetic smile.

"Come, Colonel," Lang was saying, one hand at Wolff's elbow, "we must hurry."

Wolff pulled away and craned his neck to catch another sight of Minmei; but Edwards's contingent was already leaving the bay, and she was lost in the crowd.

"Listen, Lang, I need a minute," Wolff said, up on his toes now.

Lang turned around to track Wolff's gaze, then he took hold of him more firmly, more urgently. "The council is ready to hear you. Everything hinges on this."

"Look, I just wanted to—"

"I know. I understand," Lang added after a moment. "But things have changed, man. Aren't you listening to me? Think about your friends."

Wolff started to say something rash, but checked himself, slicking back his hair in a gesture of exhaustion. "I'm sorry, Lang." He turned and motioned Janice and Sarna forward, then pointed to Burak and Tesla. "I want these two placed in lockup." Peripherally, Wolff caught Lang's look. "I'll explain," he told him.

As everyone began to move off, Lang mentioned that the Regent had come to Tirol of his own volition; that he was in fact on the fortress at that very moment.

Wolff made a surprised sound—but not half the one Tesla uttered at overhearing the statement. Wolff was too wrapped up in Lang's subsequent remarks to hear it, however; but had he turned, he would have seen the look of near rapture on the Invid's suffused face.

The Plenipotentiary Council convened in extraordinary session to listen to Colonel Wolff's report and hear out his requests. Because both Janice and Sarna were "civilians" according to the council's guidelines, Wolff had to face the twelve alone. The session was held in the council's private chambers aboard the fortress, with the usual secretaries and officials in attendance. Representing the RDF were Generals Reinhardt and Edwards. Wolff had yet to learn about Edwards's relationship with Minmei, but he loathed the man nonetheless. Lang had instructed Wolff before the session convened to meet with him afterward in the scientist's quarters. "No matter what the outcome," Lang had said. And those words were repeating themselves now as Wolff stood before the council recapping the events of the past four months.

"... But it appears that the Praxians abandoned their world for good reason," Wolff was concluding a short time later. "Praxis is unstable. Admiral Hunter—"

"I would caution Mr. Wolff from using any honorifics," one of the council members said. "The council no longer recognizes you as members of the Robotech Defense Force."

"Some of the council," Niles Obstat objected.

"*Most* of us."

Wolff scowled at the woman. "Then why aren't Janice and Sarna here, if we're all civilians?"

"Mr. Wolff," Senator Longchamps cut in, "we are just

trying to set things straight for the record. You and the Hunters, Sterlings, and Grants are understood to be a part of the Expeditionary mission. The extraterrestrial Sentinels are another matter. And as for Ms. Em, she has never been affiliated with the RDF—or the mission, for that matter, if I'm not putting too fine a point on it."

Wolff fought down an explosive urge to tear the man's throat out. "I apologize to the council if I may seem *impatient*," he continued more calmly, "but the fact is that our *friends* are out there, marooned on a planet that for all I know is just a memory by now! All I'm asking you for is *one* ship with a skeleton crew."

"To do what, Mr. Wolff?" Thurgood Stinson asked. "To rescue your friends, to be sure. But what then—continue on your campaign, or return to Tirol?"

Wolff tightened his lips. "I don't think I'm qualified to answer that, Senator."

"And we're not certain we can spare a ship just now, Mr. Wolff."

Justine Huxley broke the uncomfortable silence. "I think we're missing the point here." She motioned to Wolff. "*Friends*, is the term the colonel used. I ask you all to disregard for a moment the events of the past four months, and recall our first meeting with the Sentinels, especially the pledges that were exchanged then."

As the council members grumbled agreement in their individual fashions, Wolff caught Exedore and Lang sending hopeful looks in his direction.

Then Edwards got to his feet to address the twelve.

"I'd be the first to admit that the Sentinels are both our friends and allies," he began, "but there's an important issue here that's being neglected—the Invid. The Regent's position is very clear: any assistance we render will be considered a further act of war. And he makes no distinction between Humans and XTs in this matter."

Wolff's heart sank.

Edwards waited for the room to quiet. "I don't think it's necessary for me to remind the council of the presence of the Invid fleet. I'm not saying that if it came right down to mixing it up with them we couldn't come out on top, but the results of an engagement in any case would have disastrous effects on our long-range goal—to repair our ship and return to Earth. I'm sure General Reinhardt and Admiral Forsythe concur in this matter."

Reluctantly, Reinhardt inclined his head, averting Wolff's gaze. Edwards, however, was regarding Wolff.

"The timing couldn't be worse, Wolff. I'm sorry. Perhaps if we wait until the truce is signed—say, six months or so—"

"They don't have six months!" Wolff shouted. He looked to the council. "One ship! One goddamned—"

"The council will take these things into consideration and render its judgment in a few days, Mr. Wolff," the senator bit out, his face flushed.

"But—"

"In a few days, Wolff."

The senator's gavel went down.

"It is fate at work!" Tesla roared jubilantly. "Do you see, Burak—does it escape you how we came to be here, how we were *meant* to be here?"

Burak screwed up his devil's face and gestured to their surroundings. "Here? Meant to be here?"

Tesla made a dismissive motion. "In this ship at this particular time," he emphasized. "With the Regent close enough to touch." His hands flexed around an invisible throat.

The two conspirators were sequestered in the fortress's confinement area, opposite one another in separate laser-barred cells. Burak was sullen-faced, perched on the edge of an aluminum-framed bunk studying his hands, while across the corridor Tesla paced back and forth.

"We must find a way out of here," the Invid said, coming to a halt. "I must . . . *talk* to him, convince him—" He whirled to face Burak. "You don't think they would keep my presence from him a secret, do you?"

Burak shrugged.

"I cannot take the chance," he muttered, back in motion once more. "Burak, do you still wish to see your planet freed from its curse?"

"You know I do, Tesla. But how can I help you now? They've even taken your fruits from my care."

"Never mind the fruits." Tesla cautiously pushed his hand into the lasers' field, and winced at the resultant burn. "Just do as I ask when the moment arrives. We have not come this far to be cheated out of our victory."

Betrayal of a different sort had Minmei in tears in Edwards's quarters. The general was lying on the bed, his back against the headboard, hands clasped behind his head. Minmei was well within reach in a chair by the bed, but otherwise remote. He had found her waiting for him upon his return from the council chambers, still ruffled from her impulsive flight to the fortress, her eyes red-rimmed and swollen. He didn't need to ask; so instead, he had fixed himself a drink, kicked off his boots, and settled himself on the bed while she cried.

"He's alive," Edwards said now, reaching for the drink. "Isn't that what counts?"

She lifted her face from her hands to stare at him. "That's the problem."

"Oh, you wish he was dead."

Minmei sobbed and shook her head. "You bastard," she told him.

Edwards laughed derisively and took a long pull from the glass, determined not to give in to her. "What do you want from me, Minmei?"

She wiped her eyes and glared at him. "Is it too much to expect some support?"

"You don't need my support. You're feeling guilty because Wolff was stupid enough to think you'd just sit around and pine for him. And I suppose I don't count anymore—I was just a shoulder to cry on."

"Stop it, T.R.—please." Minmei kneeled by the bed,

resting her cheek on his thigh. "What am I going to say to him?"

Edwards made a harsh sound and pulled himself away from her sharply. He got up off the opposite side of the bed and walked to the center of the room, turning on her. "I don't have time for this kind of nonsense. Tell him whatever you want. Just quit whining about it."

He kept his back to her while he freshened his drink; but he could hear her slipping into her shoes and moving toward the door. "And tell him I said 'Hi,'" he managed before the door closed.

His hand was shaking as he downed the second drink; he was about to head for the shower when his com tone sounded. It was Major Benson.

"Some interesting conversation down in confinement," Edwards's adjutant reported. "Seems there's no love lost between Tesla and the Regent. He's pretty anxious to talk to his commander in chief, but it sounds to me like he's got murder on his mind."

Edwards's head went back in surprise. "An unexpected development."

"He's got some kind of deal going with that other alien. Can't make too much sense of it. Some payback after Tesla sets himself up as number one."

While Benson continued to fill in the scant details, Edwards concluded that an assassination might prove an advantageous event. He didn't believe the Invid fleet would go to guns over the death of an imposter—there was simply too much at stake—and by *allowing* the murder, Edwards would be sending a clear message to the real Regent. More than that, Edwards could lay the blame for a complete diplomatic breakdown on Wolff, and by extension, the rest of the Sentinels.

"Anything else from other quarters?" He heard Benson laugh shortly.

"You'll love this. I think Lang is going to offer Wolff the SDF-7. Of course Wolff would have to make it look like he pirated the thing . . ."

Edwards mulled it over. A murder, the theft of a ship, an escape . . . and the council's okay to hunt the assassins down—a chance to finish the job the Invid had begun.

Edwards smiled down on the intercom. "I'll get back to you," he told Benson.

Somewhere along the line, everyone seemed to lose sight of the fact that love had won the First Robotech War. Now it was down to ships and body counts; it was no longer a fight for survival but a war for supremacy, a savage game.

Selig Kahler, *The Tirolian Campaign*

Love is a battlefield.

Late twentieth-century song lyric

"IT'S BAD NEWS, COLONEL," DR. LANG TOLD WOLFF two hours after the council had adjourned.

They were in Lang's quarters now, along with Exedore, Janice, and the XT, Sarna. Wolff had spent the intervening time pacing the fortress's corridors like an expectant father. He had tried to locate Minmei, but no one seemed to know where she had disappeared to after leaving the docking bay with Edwards and his staff.

"The council is going to rule against you," Lang continued, passing drinks to everyone but Sarna. "Huxley and Obstat are on our side, possibly Stinson, and Reinhardt's vote counts for something, but we don't have enough to sway the rest."

Wolff scowled and sipped from his glass. "You know what's funny? In a crazy way I can see their point. You help us, and so-long any hopes of a truce."

"You're correct, Colonel," Exedore affirmed. "The Sentinels were meant to be our ally, but instead they've become our liability. And as you yourself understand, Earth's safety remains the council's primary concern. A protracted war with the Invid will only diminish our chances of intercepting the Robotech Masters."

Wolff exchanged looks with Sarna and Janice; both women seemed curiously detached from the scene, almost as if they served some unknown, greater cause. "Look," he said, putting his drink down in a gesture of finality, "now that we all understand the diplomatic angles of this thing, *how in the hell are we going to help them*!" He shot to his feet. "You think I can just sit around here, knowing what they're going through? They're *stranded* out there."

"Perhaps there is a way," Lang said after a brief silence. He shook his head back and forth. "It could have disastrous consequences, Colonel, *disastrous*. And you'd have to prepare yourselves for hardships of an entirely new order..."

Prison, Wolff thought. *As an appeasement to the Regent after the rescue*. Would Rick accept it, he wondered, or would they choose to die on Praxis—outcasts? "A ship," Lang was saying when Wolff looked up—*a ship*! He tried to follow the doctor's nervous movements as he went on to explain.

"It's one of our prototypes—not large, and not especially well-armed. But it's capable of local fold operations, Wolff, and there's a skeleton crew standing by—volunteers, each one of them loyal to the admirals."

Wolff's mouth dropped open; even Janice and Sarna were stunned by the doctor's revelation. "But when could we get it?" he asked.

Exedore turned to him. "First, Colonel, you'll be required to *steal* it."

Just then the door tone to Lang's quarters sounded. Lang looked around anxiously, then got up to answer it. A moment later, he was showing Lynn-Minmei into everyone's midst.

"Janice," Minmei said, approaching her former partner. Janice evaded Minmei's embrace, and nodded coolly.

"Lynn."

The singer began to look around the room. Lang cleared his throat meaningfully. "I think we should give Minmei and the colonel some privacy," he said, already ushering Exedore, Janice, and Sarna from the room.

When the door slid shut a moment later, it was Minmei who eased out of Jonathan's embrace. "Lynn, what's wrong?" he said, standing there with his arms open.

She fumbled with the hem of her jacket and forced a smile. "Colonel, I can't tell you how hap—"

"'Colonel'? Lynn, tell me what's going on. I saw you with General Edwards this morning and now you're calling me colonel after I haven't seen you in six months . . ." He tried to hug her once more, but she deftly took his hand between hers and motioned him to the couch.

"Jonathan," she began hesitantly, "I know you're expecting us to take up where we left off, but things have changed."

"So I keep hearing."

Wolff was suddenly defensive, and she picked up on his tone. "You have to remember, we only had a few days together. And until yesterday I thought . . ."

"You thought I was dead."

Minmei nodded. "I didn't know what to do. I was practically crazy with grief and anger." She met his gaze and held it. "I hated you, Jonathan—hated you for leaving me, hated you for . . . so many things."

Wolff considered her words, then smiled in sudden realization. "And you found someone to fill in all those lonely hours."

Minmei's eyes flashed. "Why didn't you tell me you were married?"

Wolff tried to keep his face from registering surprise. "We're separated," he said. "Besides, it never came up. I was going to tell you. It's just that everything got fouled up."

"'Blame it on the Invid,'" Minmei said, almost cracking a smile. The phrase had become something of a catch-all excuse in Tiresia. Wolff was blushing. "Listen," she told him, "I'm not angry anymore. I'm just . . . happy that all of you are alive. How are Rick and Lisa? And Max—"

"So when did you start seeing Edwards?"

Minmei stood up and stepped away from the couch, wringing her hands. "I told you: you weren't there for me, Jonathan. I needed someone to turn to."

"And you picked *Edwards*?" Wolff shook his head in amazement. "Don't you realize he's against everything we stand for? He's nothing but a self-serving, egotistical maniac."

"I won't have you talking about him like that!" Minmei said angrily. "He treated me with kindness and respect, and what's more, he's the only one interested in making peace with the Invid and putting a stop to all this madness. Not like you and the rest of those . . . *Sentinels*, tearing around space stirring things up, not giving a damn what goes on back here!"

Wolff was too numb to respond. Edwards, he thought, was like some kind of toxic spill, polluting everything he touched. Minmei had her arms folded across her chest, as though she were trying to hold herself together; her foot was tapping the floor. Wolff reached for his drink and drained the glass.

"Well, I guess there's nothing more to say, is there?"

Her lips were a thin line, trembling; then all at once she seemed to relax. "I want us to be friends, Jonathan. I've opened a kind of canteen in Tiresia, and I'd love you to see it. Will you promise to stop by?"

He regarded her as one would a memory, mulling over her performance, the scene the two of them had just played out. "Sure," he told her absently, "I'll stop by."

"There's a lot you'll be able to do here—all sorts of things. You'll see." Minmei seemed excited, like she had won a court case or something. She smiled at him from the doorway. "See you soon, okay?"

Wolff forced a smile and raised his empty glass to her. "To friendship," he offered.

She threw him a wink and stepped out.

Applause, Wolff said to himself.

While Wolff and Minmei were having their heart-to-heart and Exedore and Sarna were off somewhere discussing Haydon IV's curious history, Lang took his AI creation to his office and dumped Janice's memory into one of the lab's databanks. He scanned the android's recordings, briefly reviewing the events of the Karbarran and Praxian campaigns, but focusing in on Janice's monitorings and evaluations of the Sentinels' personnel. There was data about Veidt and Sarna, the beings from Haydon IV, that justified further analysis, and some anomalies concerning the Tiresian Rem; but for the moment Lang's main concerns were Burak and Tesla. He had found the Invid's bio-readings baffling, much different from those of the so-called scientists, and superior in some respects to the Regent himself! Moreover, the data provided suggested that Tesla was after nothing less than the Regent's throne. And apparently the Perytonian, Burak, had been assisting him in some unspecified way. Lang reminded himself to alert Wolff to these matters.

Minmei was gone by the time Lang and the others returned to the scientist's quarters, and Wolff seemed sullen, just as Lang had anticipated. There was a nearly empty brandy bottle on the low table in front of the couch.

"I want to talk about that ship, Lang," the colonel said without preamble. "When can we have it?—*steal* it, I mean."

"The sooner the better."

Wolff narrowed his eyes. "What's it going to mean to the summit?"

Lang let out his breath and traded looks with Exedore. If Wolff didn't want to mention Minmei, it was fine with him.

"We've already discussed possible scenarios with Reinhardt and Forsythe. It could set things back some, of course, but as long as we can make the Regent believe that you acted on your own, I don't think we'll be jeopardizing the truce."

Exedore concurred. "Furthermore, we think it best if you take Janice, Sarna, and Burak with you. There's no telling what the Regent might expect in the way of reprisals for our . . . *carelessness*."

"We wouldn't have it any other way," Janice chimed in, seemingly unaware of the gaps in her recent past.

"What about Tesla?" Sarna thought to ask.

Lang stroked his chin. "We've been wondering about that. He could represent a welcome chip at our bargaining table. But as I understand it, that's been his primary function all along."

Wolff snorted. "I'm not saying we couldn't get along without him, but he has been useful to us."

"Not if the Regent begins to look upon him as a traitor," Exedore saw fit to point out.

Lang thought about the data he had screened, and Tesla's ambitions. "Take him," he decided at last. "I think he'll continue to serve you. In fact, from what Janice told me of the mutiny, our Tesla seems to have his sights set on leadership of the Invid. You might be able to encourage that some, Wolff."

Wolff slapped his hands on his thighs and stood up. "What are we waiting for? What about weapons and a shuttlecraft to reach the ship?"

"That's all been arranged," Exedore told him.

"What if Edwards decides to pursue us?"

"Somehow I don't think he will," Lang speculated. "But you will be hunted. You'll have to leave Praxis and remain incommunicado for a time."

Suddenly Wolff began to feel the immensity of it all. "Can you get Burak and Tesla out of lockup without arousing suspicion?"

"I think so," Lang answered him from the com.

Wolff heard him tell the guards in the confinement area to have the two XTs brought to the laboratory for testing. Then he saw Lang's face pale.

"What is it?"

"They've already been released," Lang said. "On Colonel Wolff's request."

Elsewhere in the fortress, Burak and Tesla were moving cautiously along an empty corridor space, closing on an area that had been designated for the Regent and his retinue. Only minutes before, they had overpowered their armed escorts; it had proved as simple a matter as it had been to inveigle information concerning the location of the Regent's guest quarters. Tesla was whispering self-congratulatory praises to himself now, while Burak remained in the larger being's shadow, fearful of discovery by Human personnel.

"What are you shivering about?" Tesla said, coming around, bold and aggravated. He motioned broadly to the corridor. "Fate has cleared a path for us."

Burak had to admit that that seemed to be the case. They had seen no one since leaving confinement; in fact, it was almost as if someone were running along ahead of them, sweeping the place clean. But what Tesla didn't realize was that Burak was as frightened of fate as he was anything else. It was fate that kept his planet locked in the recurring past; fate that had gotten him into this mess to begin with . . .

"I can feel his presence," Tesla announced, stopping short. Burak bumped into him and backed up a step. Tesla appeared to be growing larger as he approached his quarry. "Soon, my friend, soon."

It dawned on Burak that the Invid had more on his mind than talk, and he wanted no part of murder. He said as much to Tesla as they approached an intersection midway along the corridor. "I—I'll wait for you here—you know, s-stand guard."

Tesla looked down at him. "Fine. You do that," he sneered, and moved off into the perpendicular corridor.

A short distance from the intersection Tesla came upon the first line of Invid sentries. Recognizing the Regent's chief scientist, they immediately genuflected and offered their salute. Then four of the Regent's elite soldiers came forward to escort Tesla into the Regent's private chambers.

"Tesla!" the simulagent gasped, spilling a lapful of fruits to the floor as he stood up. "They've released you?" His snout went up in an approximation of a laugh. "I knew I could do it!"

Tesla regarded the gesture with indifference, too caught up in the moment to realize just who and what he was dealing with.

"I have things to discuss with you, sire," he said, taking a menacing step forward.

"Yes, I'm sure you do! Tesla, I'm delighted to see you."

"We'll see," Tesla told him. "But perhaps you should reserve judgment until you've heard me out."

The simulagent's elongated brow wrinkled. There was something in Tesla's tone . . . His black eyes began to dart around the room. *The guards*, he remembered, and made a move toward the door.

"Don't even think of it," Tesla said, stepping into his path. He thrust a powerful finger into the simulagent's chest and held his other hand up for inspection. "Five fingers, Regent. *Five!* There was a time when your wife alone had five fingers. Doesn't that tell you something about me?"

At Tesla's shove, the false Regent fell backward onto a table that somehow managed to support his bulk. "Tesla, you're mad! What are you trying to do?"

"Mad? Anything but mad, Your *Highness*! I have been ingesting the fruits of other worlds, while you've been playing silly war games with these Humans. And as a result I've had my inner eye opened to transcendent realities, while you've set your gaze on meaningless conquests. I have been *evolving*, while you have sunk to your neck back into the slime that gave us birth. The fruits were meant for you, but it is *Tesla* who has reaped their subtle benefits. You used to ridicule my delvings into such things, but regard me now: I *live*, Regent," Tesla intoned, raising his arms above his head, "and you will *die* unless you abdicate to me!"

The simulagent opened his mouth to cry for help, but nothing emerged.

"Kneel before me!" Tesla demanded, gesturing to the floor.

Paralyzed with fear, the simulagent gulped and found his voice. "Tesla, listen to me: you don't understand. I—"

"Kneel before me!"

"I—"

Tesla grabbed the false Regent by the cowl and dragged him to his knees. "I will rule in your place. I will lead our race from this moment on. Do you agree to it?"

"Tesla," the simulagent pleaded. "I can't agree—"

"Fool! Would you force me to kill you!" His hands were clasped around the simulagent's thick neck now.

"—"

"Abdicate!"

"—"

"Surrender to me!"

"—"

The simulagent's four-fingered hands tore desperately at Tesla's own, but could not counter the strength madness had lent them. Tesla's powerful thumbs found soft and vulnerable places as he continued to squeeze the life from his would-be foe. Black eyes bulged and a horrible death rattle began to emerge from the simulagent's ruptured throat. Then it was over.

He withdrew his hands and stepped back, as if waking from some somnambulistic experience. The Regent's body was sprawled on the floor below him, already drained of life's vernal colors. This being, who had been like a father to him . . . And suddenly Tesla knew a gut-wrenching fear —a fear intense enough to engulf all the anger and hatred and maniacal urges he had given vent to only a moment before. He turned to the door, down in a fugitive's stoop, fluids running wild within him. He had been misguided! *He could not take the Regent's place!* The Regis would murder him for his betrayal. He would be devolved to the lowliest life-form, a mere troglodyte, exiled from his own kind. And what was he to do now? . . .

He remembered the Sentinels. Surely Wolff would be returning to Praxis, he thought. He would persuade Wolff and the others to take him along, remain with them until all this blew over. The Regis might rule for a time, but sooner or later he would assume his rightful place and rule by her side—the Sentinels would encourage him to do so!

Tesla gave a final look at the body. He began composing himself for the guards, then realized that no such charade was necessary. With the Regent dead, they were little more than mindless devices; it was possible they wouldn't even remember Tesla's visit.

With these things in mind, he opened the door.

Lang, Wolff, and the others had split up to search the fortress for Burak and Tesla, after agreeing on a time to rendezvous in the shuttle launch bay. With an all-Human crew aboard—save the Regent and his retinue—there wasn't much chance of the XTs escaping detection; but one never knew what to expect from Tesla. There was no time to investigate the release order that had freed them, either, but Lang promised to look into the matter later on.

It was Exedore who discovered Burak lurking in one of the corridors near the ship's designated Invid sector. It occurred to him that the fortress seemed unusually deserted, but he barely gave it a second thought. He was explaining the need for urgency to the Perytonian when Tesla showed up all in a rush, looking like he had just seen the face of the Creator.

"Where have you been?" Exedore said, toe-to-toe with the towering Invid.

Tesla began to stutter a response, then remembered himself and said, "I don't have to answer to some Zentraedi clone."

Exedore bristled at the comment, but decided against engaging in what would be a useless argument. Instead, he drew a handgun, informed the two of Wolff's departure plans, and hurried them along to the hold. Wolff, Janice, and Sarna were already there, anxious to get under way. The guards—some of whom were part of the plan—had already been dispatched, so it was safe for the moment for both Lang and Exedore to be on the scene.

"I guess this is good-bye for a while," Wolff was saying while Sarna and an armed Janice escorted Burak and Tesla aboard. "I don't know what to say, Lang."

"Just pray we're not too late," Lang said soberly. He offered Wolff his hand. "Godspeed, Colonel."

Wolff stepped back and saluted Lang and Exedore, gave one last look around the bay, and hastened up the ramp.

Lang said, "Have we done the right thing, Exedore?"

"We do what we can," the Zentraedi told him.

They didn't wait around to watch the launch.

"They're on their way, General," Colonel Adams reported to Edwards a short time later. "Your orders?"

"Your men are to give pursuit, but tell them to keep their enthusiasm in check. Just be sure it looks good, and make certain that the ship is allowed to fold. I don't want any slipups now."

"Roger, sir," Adams said, and signed off.

Edwards collapsed onto his bed, weary from the choreographing the plan had entailed. Freeing the aliens, supplying them with what they needed to know, keeping the corridors clear, instructing the guards in confinement and in the shuttle bay how to behave . . . It was more than most men could have handled. But then again, Edwards reminded himself, he was not *most men*.

And so far things had gone off without a wrinkle; the Invid imposter was surely dead, and Wolff was a criminal. The council could not help but see things his way from now on, and the threat of a stepped-up war with the Invid would result in the construction of the fleet he needed to carry out his more important plan: *the eventual conquest of Earth*.

SEVEN

Miriya Parino Sterling's rescue of the Spherisian crystallite [sic] was an act of derring-do worthy to stand beside the infamous "costume change" that had earned her husband such plaudits during the early stages of the First Robotech War.

LeRoy La Paz, *The Sentinels*

"I WANT SOMEONE TO SWEEP THE CAVES," RICK SAID into his helmet pickup. "Then we're out of here!"

Bela volunteered. Rick looked around and spied her down below, waving to him from the area the GMU had occupied before Cabell's desperate plan had been set in motion. Rick chinned the helmet stud again and told Bela to make it quick. He saw her, Kami, and Learna scurry off toward the mouth of the cave and disappear inside. Rick called up a display on the helmet's faceshield; then, satisfied that he had sufficient oxygen remaining, he scrambled up the steep slope toward the relocated vehicle.

Praxis's atmosphere had grown superheated and unbreathable, forcing everyone but Veidt and Teal into helmets and environment suits. From the high ground above the caverns, where the GMU was maintaining its precariously angled position, Rick glanced back at the wrinkled terrain. Eruptions of volcanic light could be seen through the dense shroud that stretched from the hills all the way to the base of a distant escarpment. And out of this storm came two lone Veritechs, returned from a final reconnaissance flight. Rick tuned into the command freak, only to have his worst fears confirmed: there wasn't a safe region to be found anywhere on the planet.

The Alphas whooshed in overhead, reconfigured, and maneuvered into the open maw of the GMU's ordnance bay. The Hovertanks and the Skull's VTs were already aboard; only two mecha remained outside—the VTs Rick and Max would pilot up once Vince Grant gave the go signal.

Rick dug his toes into the ground and completed the climb, out of breath when he reached the rim of the chute the Sentinels had blown open in the roof of the cave. The front end of the GMU overhung the rim, elevated now by the hundreds of orbs that had streamed from the cave after the chute had been opened. It was Cabell's idea, and Veidt's peculiar talents, that made the plan workable.

As a last resort the Sentinels had decided to enlarge the diameter of the cave's internal passageways to accommodate the huge creatures stuck for want of an egress suited to their size. That way, Cabell reasoned, they could at least raise a few more Alphas before the planet blew itself to smithereens—providing of course that the orbs could be made to understand that the Sentinels weren't trying to destroy them, as they had those spiderlike monstrosities. And assuming for the time being that Wolff and Janice, or *someone*, would be coming to their rescue.

Rick couldn't recall just who had pointed out that some of the larger orbs were still going to face difficulties reaching the entrance; but it was Veidt who proposed boring an artificial chimney through the roof of the cave. Additionally, the Haydonite maintained, the Sentinels were wasting their time airlifting individual mecha, when the increased supply of globe-beings would allow them to raise the entire GMU—if the mobile base could be positioned in such a way that the orbs could get underneath. (Even with its one-hundred-foot tires, the thing was still too low to accommodate the largest of the orbs.) Vince, Rick, Lisa, and some of the others had determined that the GMU could sustain itself in orbit for a limited time, thanks to the modifications the landcrawler had undergone during its stint with the *Farrago*. It would mean a dangerously uncomfortable existence for as long as Praxis held together; but even weightlessness and privation were preferable to the death they were bound to suffer on the surface.

So after Veidt had relayed the details of the scheme to the orbs (who were in his words "thankful" and more than willing to reciprocate), and firepower had opened the chute, the GMU was repositioned at the rim of the opening to catch the creatures as they levitated from the cave.

As Rick regarded the all-but-floating vehicle now, he decided it was the most bizarre sight he had ever seen: the GMU looked as though it were sitting atop a mountain of unburstable bubbles. Veidt was hovering nearby directing the flow. And in spite of the scale and the incredible size of some of the orbs, the end result of the Sentinels' partnership with the creatures had rendered the GMU almost toy-like in appearance.

Rick continued to watch in amazement as more and more orbs attached themselves to the cluster. The GMU's massive wheels were fully off the ground now, and Rick was anticipating Vince Grant's words even before they issued through the helmet speakers.

"The ride's starting, Rick. You better get the Alphas up." Grant's tone was one of excited disbelief.

Rick turned in time to see Veidt give him a knowing nod, signaling that he had "heard" Grant's message. When the Haydonite began to move off in the direction of Max's Alpha, elevating some as he hovered along the rim of the chute, Rick chinned Bela's frequency.

"A moment more," the Praxian told him. "Teal is with us."

"What's she doing down there?" Rick asked, surprised. "Everyone was supposed to be aboard by now."

"You will hear it from her own mouth," Bela told him shortly.

Rick understood that it had something to do with Baldan's death, and thought better than to press for details. "All right," he said. "Tell Kami and Learna they'll be riding with Max and Veidt. You and Teal will go up with me."

Bela acknowledged, and Rick hurried off to the Guardian-mode Alpha, which was sitting at the edge of the GMU's bubble mountain like some diminutive bird-of-prey. He threw himself up into the cockpit and brought the mecha's engines to life. Beside him the mountain was lifting off, while Praxis continued to rumble its ominous farewells.

In Fantomaspace, meanwhile, the pirated shuttle carrying Wolff and company from the SDF-3 was closing fast on the anchored dreadnought Lang had been instrumental in procuring.

"They're warning us to come about and return to the fortress," Janice told Wolff from the command seat. "Scanners show two gunships on our tail."

Wolff leaned forward to study a monitor, straining against the chair's harness. Elsewhere in the small command cabin, Sarna and Burak were similarly strapped in. Too large for any two of the shuttle's acceleration couches, Tesla was in the cargo hold, shackled but free-floating.

"Any word from the cruiser?" Wolff asked in a determined voice.

"Negative. They're not even responding to the SDF-3 bridge."

"Good. Now if we can just get there in time . . ."

A blaring sound began to wail from the control station's external speakers, and Janice swung to an adjacent console. "We're being targeted."

"Ignore it," Wolff snapped. "The first one will be a warning shot. With a little luck we'll be too close to the cruiser for them to risk a second."

"Steady. . ." Janice cautioned, and a split second later a bolt of angry light strobed into the cabinspace through the forward viewports. A second burst followed, singeing the shuttle's radome. Displays and monitors winked out, then revived.

Wolff showed the others a roguish grin. "Now we couldn't answer them if we wanted to."

"Cruiser's docking bay is opening. The bridge is patching into our guidance system. The SDF-3 thinks they're assisting in our capture."

"Let them take us in," Wolff ordered. He turned his head to take a final look at the SDF-3, suppressing a wish to see the fortress holed and derelict.

Janice straightened in her chair to obstruct his view. "The fortress is repeating the warning. Admiral Forsythe—"

"To hell with them," Wolff barked.

Four crewmembers were on hand to meet the shuttle in the docking bay. "We were attached to Major Carpenter's command," one of the young officers explained as Wolff stepped out. "Welcome aboard, sir."

Sarna hovered alongside Wolff; Janice was last out, keeping a watchful eye on Burak and Tesla.

Wolff accepted the proffered hands. "Carpenter, huh? Good man. Sorry he can't be with us."

"Dr. Lang has other plans for him, sir," an ensign supplied.

"So I understand," Wolff said. Then, as if remembering: "Listen, we've got to do something about those gun—"

"All taken care of, sir. We put a few shots across their bow and they showed their bellies."

Wolff returned a weak smile. "You know what that means, Captain—you're committed."

"We were all along. Now we can act on it."

"All right," Wolff said, nodding, his smile broadening. "Let's get under way."

As they left the bay, the ensign added, "Course is set for Praxis."

"What's our ETA?" Janice wanted to know.

"Two days relative." The captain saw their surprise. "We've made some improvements since you left."

"I guess you have," Wolff enthused. And he began to think about those improvements as the captain hurried him to the bridge. Carpenter was one lucky soul, getting a shot at returning to Earth. Wolff never would have believed he could be envious of such an opportunity, but the events of the past thirty-six hours had punched a lot of holes in his former thinking. *Things have changed*, he seemed to hear both Lang and Minmei say; and indeed they had. He would be the next to return Earthside, he decided. One way or another. And for the first time in a year he thought about the family he had left behind, and the love he would try to reawaken.

The orbs had lifted the GMU to an altitude of almost twenty miles by the time Rick and Max brought their Alphas aboard. Below, hidden beneath a swirling, agitated pall of cloud cover, Praxis was fractured beyond recognition, the molten stuff of its core geysering to the surface and boiling away the planet's oceans and fragile atmosphere. Microclimates and cyclonic storms added to the fury, unleashing blinding bolts of lightning and torrents of black rain, while volcanoes answered the skies with thunderous volleys of their own making. Praxis bellowed and roared like some tortured animal, rattling the GMU with its clamorous cries.

In the base's pressurized ordnance bay, Rick and the others began to wonder whether they would make it after all. Veidt had told them that the orbs could only remain clustered for a short time once they reached the outer edge of the planet's envelope; but with Praxis seemingly entering its final phase, the base would need to be hundreds of thousands of miles out—at least as far as the planet's primary satellite. The way Cabell saw it, the Sentinels had one recourse: to use the most fully fueled VTs and Logans to reach the far side of the moon. A preliminary count of the available mecha, however, had already pointed up the cruel truth half the Sentinels would have to face; and even so, what would the rest have accomplished outside of prolonging the inevitable? Were they to throw together a bivouac on the moon's frozen surface, or simply wander the wastes like some misguided flock until the mechas' power and life-support systems failed?

In another part of the bay, Gnea and Bela were asking Teal why she had gone back to the cave. Neither of the Praxians knew much about Spheris or the ways of its crystalline life-forms, but the women guessed that Teal would have been just as happy to have remained on Praxis with her dead comrade.

"But we've all endured losses and hardships," Bela was telling her, trying to be helpful. "Recall how Lron and Crysta suffered when the *Farrago* met its end, and how Gnea and I grieved for our Sisterhood. Now our very world . . ."

Lron, who was standing within earshot, made a kind of mournful growl. "Death is the way of the world," he muttered in the usual Karbarran fashion. "We do not mourn the loss of our friends; we are resigned to such things."

"I'm not mourning for Baldan," Teal said, looking up at him and Crysta. "I'm upset about the child."

"The dead child," Gnea started to say.

"It's not dead," Teal said harshly, standing up and walking away from them.

"It lives?" Bela said, catching up and spinning her around by the arm. "And you would knowingly abandon it?"

"Let her be, Bela," Lron cut in. "You know nothing of their ways."

"I know what it means to leave a being to die," she answered him. "Why, Teal?" she asked.

The Spherisian gazed at her coldly. "Because I will have to care for the infant. *That* is our way."

Teal snatched her arm away and Bela threw back her broad shoulders. "I will return for the child. *I* will raise it, if you won't."

Teal whirled on her, pointing a hand accusingly. "What do Praxians know of motherhood? I forbid you!"

Even Gnea had misgivings about the idea, and risked a step into Bela's path. "Think twice, Sister. Besides, it is too late—Halidarre rests and our Praxis is out of reach."

"I'll take you," a female voice rose up from the group of mecha pilots that had gathered round. Miriya Sterling eased her way her way through the group, until she was toe-to-toe with the amazon. "I'll take you," she repeated.

"A Praxian and a Zentraedi sharing the same small space?" Gnea scoffed. "Even such a mission of mercy—"

"No matter what you may think of me," the former Quadrono ace responded, "I know as much about the sanctity of life as any of you do. Give it a try, Bela—for the infant's sake." She thrust a helmet into Bela's hands.

Bela held on to the thing for a moment, then donned it, and raced with Miriya for one of the Skull's red VTs.

Rick didn't even consider trying to stop them—not that Bela or Miriya would have listened to him in any case. He had noticed a kind of latent xenophobia surfacing among the Sentinels—something stress had brought out—and reasoned that a rescue mission could provide just the rallying point everyone needed.

Bela and Miriya were suited up by the time Rick came over to wish them luck; and minutes later the bay had been cleared for the VT's launch. Miriya entered course headings as the mecha dropped down along the GMU's substantially reduced orb cluster and into the dark night of the planet's soul.

Once through the shroud, the two women witnessed for themselves the final, tormented moments of Praxis's tectonic death. Great, furious rivers of molten stuff coursed across the planet's surface now, burying forests and villages in liquid fire. Here and there, where the rivers were abruptly dammed by ground swells, were crater-sized lakes of lava, flailing white-hot tendrils into an equally hellish sky. Praxis seemed to be expanding while they watched, bursting its geological seams.

Miraculously, the region around the caves was practically unchanged, except for an expanding flow of lava that had sealed the entrance to the central cavern. The artificial chute, however, remained open and accessible.

"We'll have to go in through the top," Miriya shouted,

struggling to keep the VT stabilized in the face of intense updrafts from the liquified valley floor.

Miriya imaged the VT over to Guardian mode and dropped the mecha into a controlled fall through the wide chimney the Sentinels had blasted through fifty feet of porous rock. With external temperatures registering in the red, there was no leaving the Veritech for a personal rescue; but years of experience in handling the mecha allowed Miriya to accomplish something even more extraordinary: foot thrusters holding the mecha motionless only inches above a pool of lava that had seeped in through the mouth of the cave, she utilized the radome to rake the throbbing crystal away from the wall where Teal had dropped it. Then, when the Spherisian infant was within reach, she took it gingerly into the VT's metal-shod hand, brought up the thrusters, and took the Guardian up the chimney, in a kind of stork reversal.

All the while, Bela was offering words of encouragement, and free of the chute now, she reached forward to give Miriya an affectionate squeeze on the shoulder.

Praxis did all it could to ground the tiny craft, hurling plumes of fire at its tail and chasing it to the edge of space with savage stabs of lightning; but there was no stopping Miriya, no way she would permit the planet to reclaim the child they had rescued from its unharnessed evil.

Once more through the pall, the VT reached the deceptive safety of the planet's stratosphere. Locked on to the GMU's frequency now, Miriya and Bela began to relax some; but as they approached the ten-wheeled battlewagon and its support cluster, they saw something that delivered them to the edge of panic: both the vehicle's launch doors were wide open, and local space was littered with VTs and Logans, even half-a-dozen reconfigured Hovertanks. Miriya and Bela thought for a moment that things had reached the hopeless level, and someone had given the abandonship order, a reckless last gasp for the moon . . .

Then they spotted the dreadnought, Wolff's bright spot in the galaxy—the SDF-7 rescue vessel.

* * *

One day Rick and Lisa would compare the rescue of the Sentinels to the SDF-1's rescue of Macross from the Solar System's outer circle of frozen hell; there was the same sense of urgency, the same logistical problems and sacrifices—and chief among these would be the GMU itself. With the orbs beating a fast path for the safety of interstellar space, the Sentinels had no way to maneuver the base aboard, and there was no docking bay in the SDF-7 large enough to contain it even if they could. But just now, to everyone but Vince Grant, the GMU was of secondary concern. Distance was the crucial matter at hand—how much could be put between the cruiser and Praxis, and just how quickly.

They were close to a million miles out when the planet came apart, when enough force to obliterate the moon—the place Rick had recently seen as their possible salvation. Bela and Gnea were on the bridge to witness the brief fireball that flared where a world had once turned.

"We are homeless," Bela cried.

But from what Rick and the others were beginning to understand, the Praxians weren't the only ones. Again a comparison with the SDF-1 would present itself, the memory of a council's edict that forbade the fortress to remain the Earthspace, an edict that effectively betrayed the Robotech Defense Force. *And such betrayals*, Rick reminded himself, *had a cruel way of balancing out . . .*

Superluminal Reflex drives kept the fortress well ahead of Praxian debris, and during that brief run to the outer limits of the planetary system, Wolff related to his dazed comrades the sobering tale of his short stay aboard the SDF-3. Wolff knew nothing of the simulagent's assassination, and Tesla certainly wasn't talking; but even without that subplot, there was more than enough to leave the Humans dumbfounded.

As they continued to rehash the details, a curious understanding of the council's decision began to undermine their initial outrage. But that Wolff should have to steal a ship, and that the Sentinels would as a consequence be viewed as outlaws . . . these things were not so easily embraced. For the XT Sentinels, the revelations only meant that they had gained a second enemy instead of a much-needed ally. Among the group, however, there was the beginning of a renewed cohesiveness.

Rick thought he detected something unsettling in Wolff, but he dismissed it, speculating that he would probably have returned in even worse shape.

"Do we return to Tirol, or continue on as planned?" Rick asked everyone. "If we opt for going back, it could mean prison for most of us, death for some," he added, glancing over at Wolff. "On the other hand, it might give us a chance to explain ourselves to the council and keep Edwards from gaining any further influence."

"What do we care about your General Edwards?" Lron shouted, looking for support from the other XTs. "The Invid are our enemy. And if your forces decide to side with them against us, so be it."

Kami, Learna, Crysta, Bela, and Gnea voiced their support for Lron's position. Cabell, Rem, Janice, Sarna, and Veidt were curiously quiet.

Rick silenced them and directed the question to the RDF contingent. Lisa stood up to answer him.

"I understand the need for countering Edwards's influence," she said in a way that was aimed at Rick, "but we have to consider the broader picture. Our return could place the council in an awkward position with regard to further negotiations."

"We'll accomplish the same thing with continued acts of aggression directed against Invid-held planets," someone from the Wolff Pack pointed out. "What happens when Edwards comes gunning for us—do we fight our own forces?"

Vince Grant shot to his feet and turned on the pilot, even as Jean was trying to calm him down. "The council would never bow to the Regent's demands that we be hunted down! They'd break the truce before they'd do that—"

"Not if Edwards is running the council!"

"Waste 'em!" said a Skull pilot. "They were ready to let us die on Praxis! I say we're free agents!"

XTs and Humans cheered. Rick found himself thinking about pirates, and happened to notice Jack Baker slapping Lron on the back, while Karen raised her eyes in an imploring gesture.

"Put it to a vote," Max suggested.

Rick scanned the crowd and received nods of agreement from Lisa, Wolff, Miriya, Vince, and Cabell. "Will it be Garuda, then, or back to Tirol?" he asked loud enough to be heard above the tumult.

"*Garuda!*" came the overwhelming response.

"Then it's settled," he said, aware once more of how he had taken charge without being asked. And from across the room, Lisa's eyes burned into his own.

CHAPTER
EIGHT

I'm looking forward to Garuda in a way that has nothing to do with what I felt toward either Karbarra or Praxis. All things point to the possibility of our being able to regroup and restrengthen ourselves there, even if we will have to suit up for the visit. God knows Lisa and I need some uninterrupted time together. We spoke of dreams tonight, and made love like we haven't in far too long. It comes down to dreams in the end—holding fast to them no matter what else is thrown in your path. I want to get back to that place in my life, and Garuda sounds like it was made to order.

From the collected journals of Admiral Rick Hunter

ONCE AGAIN THE EXPEDITIONARY MISSION'S PLENI-potentiary Council found itself in extraordinary session, the third time in as many days. Ex-colonel Jonathan Wolff and his small band of rebels had stolen a prototype warship and folded from the Valivarre system, after assassinating the Invid Regent. The ruler's body had been taken back to the fleet flagship by his retinue of scientists and soldiers, who were promising a swift and violent response to the Humans' treachery. Ships under General Edwards's command had chased the pirated cruiser, but stopped short of following it into hyperspace. It was believed, although hardly certain at this point, that Wolff was returning to Praxis; but the Sentinels' next destination was anyone's guess. And if their movements were open to question, their motives were positively baffling. Edwards was arguing this very point in the council chambers now, moving through the room like a trial lawyer, his speech angry and impassioned, his reasoning all but unassailable.

"Furthermore," he said, a forefinger raised, "it's my belief that Wolff's story was a ruse. The Sentinels sent Wolff here to kill the Regent. All his talk about the destruction of the *Farrago* and the rescue mission to Praxis was engineered as a diversion."

"That's arrant nonsense," Lang objected, getting to his feet and turning to face the rest of his group. "It was the Regent who first informed us of the destruction of the ship—"

"They *allowed* his troops to destroy the ship," Edwards cut in, but Thurgood Stinson quickly waved him silent.

"What's more," Lang said after settling his gaze on Edwards, "the Sentinels had no way of knowing the Regent's fleet was here."

Edwards laughed. "Need I point out that they could have been monitoring our transmissions, even while remaining incommunicado?"

"But to what *end*, General?" Lang asked. "Why would they knowingly sabotage the negotiations? Really, this makes no sense whatsoever, and I would caution the council to understand that General Edwards is offering us nothing more than an *interpretation* of the facts."

"The facts, Doctor, are that the Regent is dead and one of our ships has been stolen. What more do you require?"

Tight-lipped, Lang took his seat. Senator Longchamps cleared his throat meaningfully. "The council appreciates Dr. Lang's reminder, but I for one would like to hear the general's assessment of the Sentinels' motives."

Edwards sat in silence for a moment, then stood up and said, "They've become a private army. They've liberated Karbarra—Praxis, for all we know—and their plan is to continue in this vein until the entire local group is theirs to command. In the meantime, our efforts here will have been neatly undermined. The Invid will return in force and in the end it will be the Sentinels who will rescue us."

"This is too much," Justine Huxley interjected. "Admiral Hunter would never stoop to such measures."

"Then why did he resign his command?" Edwards threw back at her. "And why is it that the whole RDF apparat decided to follow his lead." Edwards enumerated on his fingers: "The Skull, the Wolff Pack, Vince and Jean Grant, even the Tiresian, Cabell. Hunter didn't like the idea of answering to the council's demands, and now he's out for himself."

Edwards returned to his chair, leaving the council members to argue among themselves. In the seat adjacent, General Reinhardt wore a look of complete disgust.

After a few minutes of deliberation, Longchamps announced, "The council is not yet fully convinced of the scenario you detail, General Edwards, nor of your interpretations of the Sentinels' 'master plan,' if you will."

Edwards scowled, waiting for the senator to continue.

"However, the fact remains that the actions of ex-Colonel Wolff, whatever their motivation, have placed us in a serious predicament. The council wishes to know if the Invid commanders have indicated to you any steps that can be taken to offset this injustice."

Edwards stood up, suppressing a self-satisfied grin. "Right now they seem willing to accept the facts just as we've presented them: Wolff acted on his own. But I must include this caveat: these are relatively low-echelon personnel we're dealing with, and I'm certain that once the Regis hears of this, we'll see renewed fighting—perhaps on a scale more reminiscent of the Robotech War than anything we've experienced here."

He waited for this to sink in before continuing. "As for what we can do, I would suggest that short of a preemptive strike against their forces right now, or the capture of the Sentinels, we devote all our efforts to the construction of a fleet of ships to rival their own."

Again, there were arguments and objections from various council members, but Longchamps silenced these with his gavel. "Would you be willing to oversee this project, General, if the council so votes?"

Edwards inclined his head slightly. "I would be honored, Senator. Of course, I would require the full cooperation of Dr. Lang's Robotech teams and control of the mining operations on Fantoma."

"Naturally," Longchamps said. "We will adjourn to consider our decision."

Edwards grinned in spite of himself. He shifted his gaze slightly to show Lang the cold hostility in his eye. Lang tried to return it, but could not.

The round had gone to Edwards.

In his hive complex on Optera, the Invid Regent sat alone with his two pet Hellcats, too stunned by the reports of his simulagent's murder to speak. He held his snaillike head in his hands, sunk deep into a sense of despair that was entirely new to him. Once before he had experienced such torment: when his wife had confessed to him her love for Zor. *Betrayal*, he thought, in the soft glow of the room's commo sphere.

"Your Highness, shall I give the order to attack?" a lieutenant repeated cautiously.

The Regent regarded the soldier's image in the sphere and sighed heavily. "No," he answered quietly. "Return the fleet to Optera, and tell no one that I live. It may benefit me to remain hidden for a while longer."

"But, Your Highness, are the Humans to go unpunished? And what of Tesla?"

The Regent could feel the lieutenant's anger, and it was enough to refresh him momentarily. He had not been completely abandoned, then; *loyalty* still lived.

"For the moment do nothing more than let our intentions be known. Inform the Human high command that we hold them responsible for the . . . Regent's death, and that terms for a cease-fire will not be discussed until the Sentinels have been brought to justice."

"My liege," the lieutenant returned with a note of reluctance. He offered salute and shut down the link.

The Regent placed a hand on the horned shoulder of one of the Inorganics, on its haunches beside his chair. "My pet," he said aloud, "will you, too, betray me someday?"

Tesla had murdered.

He found it almost inconceivable. Had the Sentinels put him up to it somehow, or, worse still, the Regis? They were known to have seen one another on Praxis . . . Had she promised him something then, her favorite son? Certainly Tesla had undergone some sort of change, if he was to believe the words of the simulagent's guards. Perhaps he and the Regis had made a pact to rule in his place, and as a sign of good faith she had *evolved* him some. On Praxis? he wondered. Had she gone there to carry on with her dangerous Genesis Pit experiments? He would know soon enough, if her ships suddenly showed up in Opteraspace.

But in the meantime the Regent thought it best to allow the Humans to go on thinking that one of their own had assassinated the simulagent. If, as they maintained, the group had acted alone, it showed a definite carelessness on the council's part. But if this Edwards had permitted it to happen—even *engineered* it, as the Regent was inclined to believe—then the murder had more sinister implications. It was as if Edwards knew all along that the Regent had sent an imposter in his place, and the murder was the Human's way of responding to the substitution.

He made a note to treat Edwards differently the next time.

The simulagent hadn't been able to learn anything about the Masters' destination, or the location of the Humans' *Earth*; but it was possible that his death would have a positive side effect. Obviously the Humans were anxious to sue for peace, and although he couldn't grant them this just yet, that fact eased his concern about their presence in the Quadrant. And now it was likely that others besides Edwards would be willing to turn against the Sentinels.

The Regent called up a starmap in the sphere and leaned forward to study it. "Garuda," he decided after a moment, that's where they would be heading. A miserable world if there ever was one, a world that had its own way of dealing with intruders . . . The Regent had recalled all of his warships from the planet to strengthen the fleet he had sent to Optera; but there was still a small garrison of soldiers and scientists there tending the orchards and farms and supervising the transport of the nutrient. Sufficiently fore-warned, they just might be able to succeed where larg-er forces had failed.

The Regent rubbed his hands together in a gesture of renewed excitement. He grunted to the beasts that flanked his chair. *Perhaps it wasn't so bad being dead after all*.

When news of the Plenipotentiary Council's decision was released, the Expeditionary mission found itself more divided than ever. Everyone on Base Tirol and aboard the SDF-3 now felt compelled to take a stand. The council, by majority if not by unanimous decision, had effectively branded former admirals Hunter and Hayes, along with the rest of the Human and XT Sentinels, outlaws. In due time a ship would be detailed for their capture, but presently they were to receive no help from RDF personnel, and anyone found aiding or abetting the Sentinels' cause would be subject to prosecution to the full extent of the law. Moreover, General Edwards was being placed in full com-mand of the RFD; he would be overseeing both the mining op and construction projects, and his staff would be super-vising all aspects of civil defense, including minor police actions.

Lang, Exedore, Huxley, Obstat, Reinhardt and a few others had become a cabal overnight, and Lang realized that it wouldn't be long before Edwards's Ghost Riders would be keeping watch on their every move—if in fact this wasn't already the case. There were enough unan-swered questions about the Regent's assassination to con-vince Lang that Edwards had had a hand in the affair. He surmised, too, that Edwards was aware of the assistance Lang had rendered Wolff; but if he had any proof, he was probably saving it for the next occasion the two men went toe-to-toe. Lang could only hope that Wolff had reached Praxis in time to rescue the Sentinels, because in every other way, the plan had done more harm than good. How-ever, by taking such a hard-line stance, the council had inadvertently weakened Edwards—perhaps not now, but in the long run, when those loyal to Hunter would step forward in a show of strength.

Lang was in his quarters, compiling a mental list of the men and women who could be counted on, when the door tone sounded and Lynn-Minmei begged entry. She was the last person Lang wanted to see, but as he thought about her a plan came to mind. He had persuaded her once into accepting Janice as her partner; now perhaps he could talk her into assuming the android's role as a spy.

"Dr. Lang, I hope I'm not disturbing you," she said, coming through the door. "I just had to talk to someone."

He could see she was frantic. "Don't be silly, my dear. Sit down. Can I fix you something?"

"No," she said absently. "No, thank you. I just need to know if it's true, Dr. Lang—what they're saying about Jonathan and Rick."

Lang sat down, even though Minmei remained standing. "What do you think, Minmei?"

She threw her hands up in a nervous gesture. "I don't know what to think! General Edwards says one thing, you say another..." She looked directly at him. "Most of my old friends won't even talk to me anymore. And the way Janice acted..."

He offered her an understanding nod. "Well, maybe you've just ended up on the wrong side somehow. And everyone's waiting for you to return."

She sat down, facing him. "That's what I want to know: am I on the wrong side? People are saying the most horrible things about General Edwards. But I know him, I know what kind of man he is."

"You may think you know him, Minmei, but I assure you, you don't. It's..." Lang fumbled for the words, "it's as though he has some sort of personal vendetta against Rick. I can't even begin to understand it. I only know that he has turned the council against your friends, and I know they'd be crushed to learn that you're not supporting them."

Minmei bit her lip. "And that's just what Jonathan's going to tell them, too."

Lang thought he detected a flash of anger behind the words; he started to reply, but she cut him off, the anger visible now.

"That snake! Who is he to be calling people names? He's a *liar*!"

"Minmei—"

"Mr. Charm," she said, getting up from the couch. "He should talk about *loyalty*. Ha! What does he know about anything?" She shot Lang a look. "What do any of you know?"

Lang was never good at dealing with theatrics; he knew this much about himself and kept still.

"Liars, murderers, *outlaws*," Minmei was saying. "Things were just too *peaceful* for them on Tirol. They needed to go find themselves a war."

"That's Edwards talking," Lang managed.

"This is *me* talking!" she screamed at him. "I hate you! I hate the whole bunch of you!"

She began to cry into her hands. Lang made a move toward her, but she was gone by the time he reached the door.

"Go ahead, say it," Rick said to Lisa. "I could feel you saying it clear across the hold. So let's clear the air."

She looked at him and frowned. "What are you talking about? Say what?"

They were in the small cabinspace that had been set aside as their quarters aboard the SDF-7. The dreadnought was approaching Garuda from the far side of the planet's massive sun after a brief period in hyperspace.

"You wanna say 'I told you so,'" Rick continued. "Edwards is getting stronger and now we're in no position to stop him. If we had remained on Tirol, all this would never have happened, and we'd probably have a truce worked out and be a long way toward repairing the SDF-3." Rick snorted. "Anything I've left out?"

"I'm not saying a word, Rick," she told him. "You're doing such a fine job without me."

"All right, so you think I made a big mistake, and maybe a part of me agrees with you. But the truth is that I would have been going out of my skull back there, and at least now I feel we *are* accomplishing something—maybe not for ourselves exactly, but for Lron and Crysta and Kami and everyone. You can't argue with that."

Lisa shrugged. "Who's arguing?"

"And another thing." Rick put his hands to his hips. "You figure that just because I'm suddenly all gung ho and take-charge that I really *am* a commander after all. But I'll tell you something: the only reason I'm okay with the role is because there's no damned council telling me what to think. We've got a democracy here, not some red-tape portable government, and that suits me fine."

"Well, I—"

"So don't go thinking that I'm going to ask to be reinstated when all this blows over."

"Do you think it will, Rick?"

He heard the desperation in her tone and it took the wind right out of his sails. He leaned over, took her hand, and kissed it. "You bet," he said softly. "And we'll get back on course."

She reached out to stroke his arm. "I don't want us to grow apart, Rick, and I feel that happening sometimes."

He was tempted to say something about Lisa's involvement with Gnea and Bela, but held his tongue. "I won't let that happen."

She sighed fretfully. "We used to have so many dreams —remember?"

"Of course I remember," he said, trying to sound cheerful. "And we'll make every one of them come true." He squatted down to face her. "Look, let's just see what happens on Garuda. From what Kami says, the Invid never actually conquered the place. And from what Wolff told me, it sounds like they pulled all their troop carriers away. They've got a small garrison there, and that's it. Maybe there won't have to be much fighting. We'll get to have some PT."

She laughed lightly. "Now *there's* a dream if I ever heard one."

"You'll see," he said, bringing her up into his embrace.

In the cruiser's med room, Jean Grant was trying to figure out what to do with the now-smooth, football-sized crystal on the gurney—the Spherisian infant Miriya and Bela had brought up from Praxis. The two women were watching Jean's every move, while Teal sat quietly in a corner of the room. Jean gave the crystal a gentle turn; it felt cool to the touch and seemingly inanimate, but scans had indicated a high level of bioenergy, or at least an approximation thereof. *God knew the thing was growing fast enough!* Jean sensed Miriya and Bela's eyes on her and said, "Well, what do you two expect me to do with this, this . . . *child*?" She turned sharply to Teal. "Teal, get over here! At least tell me what I'm supposed to do."

Wearily, Teal got to her feet and joined Jean at the gurney. She glanced down at the crystal and fixed her transparent eyes on the infant's saviors. "You saved him, Bela. *You* raise him."

"It's a him?" Jean asked, peering at the crystal as though she had missed something. "How do you know that?"

"Because it is Baldan's child. It is Baldan."

Miriya made a face. "Wait a minute, let's get this straight: is it Baldan, or is it Baldan's child?"

"It is both," Teal told her.

"Well, it sure doesn't look like Baldan," Jean pointed out. "Is it, er, *he* in a state of gestation inside the crystal? Or do we need to incubate him? Speak to me, girl!"

Teal turned away from the gurney. "I don't want to care for it!" When she faced them again, it was obvious she was, in some Spherisian fashion, *crying*. "Baldan was not my mate," she explained. "It was the Invid Tesla who chose us, it was he who brought us together."

Jean put a hand on Teal's shoulder. "But I don't understand, honey. What does all this have to do with caring for the child?"

"He must be *shaped*," Teal answered her. "And to do so I must enter into a rapport with Baldan—I must become his mate."

No one said anything for a moment. "And if we do nothing?" Bela asked.

"Baldan will die." Teal continued to cry, muttering to herself in her own tongue—*praying*, Jean ventured. Then suddenly she produced a kind of crystalline paring knife from the bodice of her garment.

"Teal, no!" Jean started to say, but before she could stop her, Teal had struck the infant with the edge of the blade, as one might bring a tool to bear on a piece of ore. A chip broke away from the crystal, revealing a dazzling facet. Teal struck again and again, each stroke sure of its mark, each rendering the inanimate thing gemlike and complete. Crying all the while, Teal took the infant in her hands and began to carve away more of its extraneous crust. Miriya, Bela, and Jean could hardly believe their eyes when a polished face slowly emerged, then a miniature torso of sorts.

It was Baldan.

If the Sentinels remained divided on any one issue, it was what was to be done with Tesla. While certain they would exercise more caution the next time the Invid volunteered for a mission, they had as yet no clear-cut policy toward him. Was he a prisoner, a hostage, perhaps an ally in some sense? After the meeting in which the Sentinels' direction had been put to a vote, Tesla and Burak had had a chance to answer the "charges" Wolff brought against them. They were accomplices, Wolff maintained, in the laconic and cynical fashion that had everyone aboard guessing. (That Minmei was the cause of Wolff's distress was no secret, but he kept to himself the fact that she had been seeing Edwards.)

Tesla didn't deny that he had tried to commandeer the module; his actions, however, had not been directed against the Sentinels. In fact, quite the contrary. "I am your comrade in this war of liberation," he told the Human and XT assembly. "I am as eager for peace as the rest of you, and my aim in taking over the ship was simply to speed to Optera to convince the Regent of the error of his ways."

Burak, though, was innocent to hear Tesla tell it, and had merely been overpowered, as Janice had. And much to Tesla's surprise, Janice backed up the story. But what Tesla didn't realize was that Janice had briefed the Sentinels beforehand on the stand she would take, suggesting that they allow Burak and Tesla their partnership, which she herself would monitor. There was more here than met the eye, she had explained; and the arrangement would have the added benefit of keeping the Perytonian out of everyone's way.

This was the voice of Lang's reprogramming, but no one recognized it as such, least of all Janice. Tesla, Lang had established, was worthy of study.

So in the end it was decided that things would remain much as they had been before the attempted mutiny: Tesla was neither prisoner nor ally, but more in the way of "ambassador." And Burak was to remain the Invid's aide/jailer/keeper.

The two XTs were in one of the ship's cargo holds now, a place well-suited to Tesla's size. Only a few morsels of fruit remained, but Tesla knew that more would be available to him on Garuda—a crop as different from the Praxian variety as those had been from the Karbarran. He still hadn't gotten over his case of the guilts, and was in fear of the moment the Sentinels learned of the Regent's assassination. With luck, though, that news could be months off. The beauty of it was that there was no one who could even tie him to the act—not as long as the SDF-7 remained incommunicado. Even that litle Zentraedi, Exedore, would have no proof. "Circumstantial" was the Human word for such evidence. So in spite of his anxiety, his spirits had improved.

Burak's, however, had not. Although pleased (albeit baffled) that he had been absolved of any wrongdoing, he felt as though the Sentinels had simply dismissed him and Peryton's cause.

"You mustn't be so glum about it, my friend," Tesla told him, while he contemplated one of the tidbits. "Your world is as good as freed."

"What makes you so certain?" Burak asked, his face a true devil's mask now.

Tesla popped the fruit into his mouth. "Because . . . I sense something wonderful is about to happen."

Burak regarded him with a frown.

"Truly," Tesla continued. "You must have faith if you are to assume your proper place in this world. There may be one or two dark spots in our future, but afterward . . ." Tesla offered an approximation of a smile.

"But what about *now*, Tesla? All these grand events you speak of—they are always one step ahead of us."

Tesla threw back his shoulders. "No, my young friend, you have it backward. It is *we* who are one step ahead. But change is in the air. Soon the reshapings will catch up with us. And then we can begin to transform the world."

CHAPTER
NINE

A footnote in Kahler's work (The Tirolian Compaign, Fanto-madiscs, third issue, 2083, scr. 1099) refers those interested in Garudan psychism [sic] to a series of twentieth-century auto-biographical novels written by a young anthropologist recording his attempts to enter into various states of altered reality through the guidance of an Yaqui Indian "man of power." And while La Paz is willing to concede that there is some justification for Kahler's recommendation, he points out that the Garudans required nothing in the way of extrinsic agents to attain "non-ordinary states." Unless, however, one views the planet's atmosphere in this regard. It is hoped that the much-awaited translations of Haydon's texts will shed light on this continuing controversy.

Taken from the "Imminent Immaterial" column of *Psychophysics Digest*

GARUDA. KAMI AND LEARNA HAD TOLD THEM WHAT to expect. A mostly cold and barren world of steppes and tundra, with vast frozen regions and glaciated mountain ranges. What little there was in the way of flora and fauna was principally confined to a narrow band of equatorial forestland of evergreen analogues. There were two seasons, wet and dry; Garuda was in the latter now, and that, Kami explained, would account for the differences in fur coloration the Sentinels would notice among members of his and Learna's tribe. The Garudans, who numbered in the thousands, were not, generally speaking, offworlders. Some, however, had volunteered for mining work on Rhestad-system moons after the arrival of the Zentraedi generations ago, and later on, the Masters' clones. But most Garudans feared the thought of having to leave the planet, and had little tolerance for the breathing harnesses life anywhere else would require. Their society was a simple one, organized along the lines of any hunter-gatherer group; however, they were anything but nomadic, and kept domesticated animals and raised some crops. Religion was of a decidedly individual variety, with each clan answering to a different totem, and each member his or her own shaman. Oddly enough, neither Kami nor Learna had the slightest knowledge of history in the sense that most of the Sentinels, including Burak and Lron, understood the term. Unlike the Karbarrans, or Praxians for that matter, the Garudans seemed to live entirely in the present. This is not to say that they were a complacent group—they were certainly devoted to securing a free future for their world— but at the same time, they could supply no answers to questions concerning their racial past.

This enigma had become something of a preoccupation with Cabell during the four months the Sentinels had remained grounded on Praxis. Cabell was different than the Masters in this regard. Those who had ousted the Tirolian regime after the Great Transition were more interested in expansion and conquest than in the accumulation of knowledge; to the Elders and their subordinate Triumvirates, knowledge of the past presented something of an impediment to change. They had their gaze fixed on the day after tomorrow, on issues of uncontested rule, ultimate power, and selective immortality.

The rest of the Sentinels, though, saw Garuda more in terms of its tangible challenges, and foremost among these was its very atmosphere: though Earthlike in composition, it was essentially toxic to all but the planet's indigenous life-forms. There were one or two exceptions to this, but only Veidt and Sarna among the Sentinels qualified. Surface scans verified the presence of dozens of varieties of airborne spores and microorganisms whose chemistry Jean Grant likened to certain laboratory-produced psychotropic drugs. According to Cabell—based on what he had gleaned from Zor's notes—the vulpine beings' mental processes were linked to the planet itself in a kind of submolecular partnership. Life-forms incapable of entering into this long-established microcosmic symbiosis were not, however, simply ignored or exempted; rather, they were sensed as potentially disturbing to the ecological balance and consequently *counterattacked* by those same microorganisms responsible for the Garudans' nonordinary psychic states.

It had therefore fallen upon the med group to outfit the landing party with transpirators and resp canisters. But if logistics was about to hamper the operation's effectiveness, the Sentinels could take some comfort in the fact that the Invid had also fallen prey to the planet's proprietary nature. In fact, their presence on Garuda was essentially restricted to the hemispherically shaped hives they had erected in those areas where Zor's Flower of Life seedlings had taken root. The crop was a mutant but bountiful one, and it was believed that Garuda provided largely defoliated Optera with much of its needed supply of nutrient. With Karbarra liberated, the Regent had lost his mecha factories; now the Sentinels meant to strike him at the gut level, destroying as many of Garuda's orchards and "farms" as they could.

Rick, Lisa, Cabell, Rem, Jack, Karen, Burak, Kami, Learna, Gnea, Lron, and Crysta made up the drop group, with members of the Skull and Wolff Pack escorting the shuttle down. The SDF-7 would remain in orbit to deal with Invid transport vessels, known to make frequent runs between Garuda and Optera. Wolff and Grant shared the fortress command. Janice would be keeping an eye on Tesla. Veidt and Sarna had elected to stay behind, and Bela was apparently determined to help Teal with the infant Baldan.

The landing party was certain that the SDF-7's arrival in Garudaspace had not gone undetected by the Invid; the shuttle landing would probably be monitored as well. So rather than risk immediate engagement or present any of the hives with an easy target, they opted to put down in the relatively unpoliced tribal sectors, close to Kami and Learna's village. Unexpectedly, they found themselves encircled by battle-ready troops nevertheless—even before the shuttle's landing gear made contact with the surface.

Kami had neglected to mention that some of Garuda's protectors were Tirolian Bioroids.

Kami and Learna consequently made certain they were the first to deplane, figuring their mere appearance would defuse the situation. It did so—and more. Within minutes, half of Kami's tribe had emerged from the trees to surround the shuttle and celebrate the return of their friends. The air was suddenly charged with joyous sounds—excited barking to Rick's ears—and Kami and Learna were embraced, jostled, and hoisted up on countless shoulders. With elaborate ritual, the two returnees threw off their breathing gear and pranced about, engaging in impromptu dances, shamanic steps of power.

Rick radioed the Skull and Wolff contingents to put down along the perimeter of the shuttle's rough strip, checked the integrity of his environment suit and transpirator, and followed Lisa out of the pilots' cabin to take part in the merriment. An hour later, he and the rest of the landing party were in the village's wooden longhouse powwowing with the leaders of Kami's tribe. Severed heads of Hellcats, Scrim, and Odeon Inorganics dangled from the roof tie-beams.

Also present were a number of the Bioroid pilot clones —androgynous-looking shaggy-haired humanoids with pointed features and exotic eyes. One of the clones—these Tiresian lost boys—was explaining to Cabell in a nasal, almost synthesized voice how they had come to ally themselves with the Garudan cause. They wore no breathing gear, and were apparently immune to the spores.

"The Masters left us here to police this world. But when the Invid arrived, communication with Tirol and the clonemasters became impossible. Our Hoverships destroyed, all ties with Tirol cut, we began to understand the concept of freedom, the loneliness that springs from abandonment . . ."

"So you joined the Garudans in their fight," Cabell finished, astonished.

"We thirst for freedom, just as they do."

"Remarkable," the old man mused, his own voice distorted by the mask's filters. "Absolutely remarkable." He hadn't been so astounded since learning from Lang that Miriya Parino had borne a child; and the revelation gave him some hope that the Masters' clones were actually capable of revolt.

Rick took advantage of a momentary silence to motion to the trophy heads. "What's the situation here? Do the Invid run patrols through this sector?"

The tribal chief answered him. "Their Inorganics patrol, but only when they wish to intimidate us, or gather up laborers for the farms. They don't seem to regard us as a threat—even with the firepower our comrades supply," he added, indicating the clones, "but I assure you that all Garuda is ripe for rebellion."

"You mean, they're using your people on the farms?"

"Lately, yes. And in the labor camps near them."

Lron and Crystal grunted, alarming some of the Garudans present. They were keeping a wide circle around the ursine XTs, and a wider one yet around Burak, whose mask only added to an already demonic aspect.

Rick could see that the news came as a shock to Kami and Learna also.

"So much for surgical strikes from the ship," Max said.

Rick regarded the chief for a moment. He found that he was not yet accustomed to seeing Garudans without their breathers; omnivores they might be, but there was a ferocity to their muzzles he wasn't all that comfortable with. Outwardly, the chief resembled Kami, but there was a solemnness to his aspect that was absent in the younger Garudan.

"What about mecha?" Lisa wanted to know. "Scouts, Shock Troopers?"

"Only when their transport ships arrive," the chief told her. "They patrol near the farms to protect the nutrient shipment while it is being loaded. Rarely do they venture into tribal sectors."

Rick watched the chief gnaw at a hunk of meat one of

the women had offered him. "Is there any regularity to the shipments?"

The chief exchanged a few sentences with Kami in the Garudan tongue. The Sentinel translated. "Approximately every three standard months. "This was changed every so often in an attempt to foil what was an extensive underground network at work on Garuda. But the Invid never managed to keep anything secret for very long.

"And when did the last shipment leave?"

"One month ago."

Rick grinned beneath his transpirator mask. "That means we're in the clear for the moment. Even if they've already communicated with their fleet, reinforcements could take weeks to get here."

"The closest farm is about one hundred miles from here," Learna said, without being asked. "Kami and I know that area well."

"An aerial recon," Max suggested.

"No," Rick said. "I don't think we should tip our hand just yet. We'll go in on Hovercycles first. Take a quick look around before we plan an assault. Just because mecha haven't been observed doesn't mean they're not in there."

"I agree," Rick heard Jack say behind him.

Karen nudged Jack with her elbow for butting in. "Sir?" she then said to Lisa, hoping Jack would learn by example.

"Go ahead, Karen."

"I was just wondering what exactly happened to the first Invid troops that landed here—before the hives were built, I mean."

Again, Kami and the chief exchanged a few words.

"They went mad," the Garudan leader said evenly. "Then they died."

The recon team—Rick, Lisa, Jack, Karen, Rem, and Kami as scout—left the village shortly before dawn, sticking close to the northern fringe of Garuda's preternaturally quiet forest. They had traveled seventy-five miles by the time Rhestad rose—a massive oblate field of crimson that did little to warm the land. The two villages they passed en route had already been informed of the mission. Worried about attracting any undue attention to themselves, Rick had requested that the Garudans simply go about their business; but there was obviously too much excitement in the air for that. For sometimes miles at a stretch, Rick would see them crouched along the paths the Hovercycs cut through the woods, silent and feral, vulpine eyes aglow in the eerie morning light.

At mile eighty-five the team encountered its first Inorganic patrol—a pack of Hellcats a dozen strong, roaming the forest like some fiendish pride of saber-tooths. Kami had spotted them and passed the word; the Hovercycles were shut down and concealed. It was understood by now that the Inorganics were more than marauders or Robopolice units; they functioned as the remote eyes and ears for the Invid living computers, which in turn directed the scientists or command troops. Engagement, therefore, even if it ended in victory, would have only served to alert the hive to the team's position; so they lay as still as they could, pressed close to the chilled ground until the pack had moved through.

Rick and Lisa were on their stomachs, side-by-side, environmental suits adjusted to mimic the colors and textures of the area's fernlike ground cover. Rick had his arm flung protectively across his wife's back, and was gazing at her through the helmet's bubble-shield. Her eyes returned the wrinkled look his own were trying to convey. It was the first time he and Lisa had been out together in a long while, and if this wasn't exactly anyone's idea of an ideal date or the "closeness" Lisa had in mind during their most recent heart-to-heart, at least they were together. And somehow—though Rick would have been at a loss to explain it—he felt more assured with Lisa beside him. At the same time her presence had a kind of calming effect, because no matter what they might have to face, he was freed from having to worry about where she was or what dangers she might have otherwise been facing alone. Here, he had some measure of control over her situation—*their* situation.

Moving more cautiously after Kami gave the all-clear sign, the team took another hour to cover the last fifteen miles. They had portions of the enormous hive in sight for five of those miles, but didn't get an unobstructed view of the thing until they were almost on top of it. It sat in the center of an ancient impact crater, in a veritable forest of Optera trees, a dome-shaped structure with a base almost ten miles around, composed entirely of what appeared to be organic facets or geodesics; in fact, the hive had the look of something *grown* rather than erected. Four mile-high cattaillike antenna towers were positioned at cardinal points around the hive's oddly "bubbled" base.

Through field glasses, Rick could discern Garudan slaves gathering mutated fruits from the trees. Huge containers of these were being conveyed to the hive itself by Invid soldiers in specially outfitted suits, often piloting Hovercarts of various design. Tracking the carts' movements ultimately enabled Rick to discover one of the hive's tunnellike transport corridors.

"What happens later on?" Rick whispered to Kami, who had stooped down to ask for the binoculars. "Are the workers taken into the hive?"

"No," he said, bringing his muzzle close to the helmet's audio pickups. "The labor camp lies about two miles from here." Kami pointed out the direction.

"Are you certain there are no Garudans inside the hive?"

Kami shook his head. "Not certain." The hives were the only places on the planet impervious to Garudan Sendings and out-of-body flights; but the Invids' continued presence onworld in general had confused things. The clouds and wind were full of sinister whisperings.

"Then we've gotta find out," Rick said, turning around to motion the others forward.

Jack remained behind as rear guard, while the rest of the team began to work their way over the low ridge that was the crater's rim and down into the basin itself. It was warmer here, Rick realized without having to check the suit's sensor displays; redolent, too, he imagined, as the Optera tree forests on Praxis had been. They were closing on the edge of the cultivation area now, and it was time for Kami to go it alone.

"Don't take any chances," Rick cautioned him. He checked his chronometer. "One hour. If you're not back by then, we're moving out."

"I'll get word back to you from the camp if anything happens."

The underground, Rick reminded himself.

"Just see that it doesn't," Rem said.

Karen and Lisa wished Kami luck, and he started to move off.

Then all at once a small mountain was growing under their feet. Rick thought for a moment that this might be how the bulb-canopied Optera trees pushed themselves from the ground. Lisa and the others had been knocked off their feet, but he was still riding the rise up, arms outstretched like a high-wire walker. Elsewhere he could see two more humps beginning to form. Kami yelled something incomprehensible, just before Rick leaped and caught hold of a network of vinelike tendrils encasing the canopy-bulb of the nearest tree. He was dangling ten feet above the ground now, looking down on his teammates and wondering why they had their weapons drawn, when a triple-clawed Scout pincer suddenly slammed into the tree not a foot from his head. The bulb split open like an overripe melon, showering him with viscous green gop and what he took to be seeds.

Lisa and Karen, meanwhile, were firing charges at the crab-ship, trying to position themselves for a shot at the mecha's scanner, a pouting red mouth low down on the ventral surface of its armored head. But the Scouts who had joined the first were advancing, and the two women were forced to hurl themselves out from under a pair of cloven feet. One mecha was stomping the ground, trying to pulverize them, even while Rem and Kami were stinging its ladybug-shaped carapace with Wolverine fire.

Rick disentangled himself before the first Scout could strike again, dropping, tucking, and rolling out of harm's way, and somehow managing to come up with his weapon raised. He nailed his giant assailant in the knee joint and brought it down in an earsplitting crasn; then put a second shot through its scanner, and ducked for cover as the thing blew up.

The force of the blast threw one of the other Scouts hard against the trees, where it stumbled and fell after ripping open half-a-dozen bulbs. Rem saw to it that the ship didn't get up, lancing it open from crotch to scanner. Rick had been left dazed and temporarily deaf from the explosion, but he came to in time to see the remaining mecha raising its left foot to smash Karen and Lisa, who had also been leveled by the blast. He ran up behind the Scout, as if preparing to clip it behind the knee, and emptied his handgun straight up into the underside of the ship's rear tapered head armor, eliciting a cascade of energy bolts and a muffled roar that decapitated the ship, spilling its Invid pilot to the ground. Kami and Karen holed the creature, even though it was probably already dead, and moved quickly to Lisa's side. Rick did likewise, suddenly terror-stricken. Her suit was torn open; she was bloodied and unconscious.

"We've got to get her back to the cycs!" Rick said, looking up at his teammates. But all he got in return was a look of resignation. Rick saw Kami and Karen toss their weapons aside. He whirled around, still in a crouch, in time to see more than a dozen Invid soldiers emerging from the orchard to surround their patch of green-stained ground.

"Throw your weapon down," one of the Praxian-size soldiers said in Tiresian, brandishing an evil-looking rifle/cannon and gazing down at Rick through an elongated helmet.

Rick did so, just as an officer came shouldering its way through the circle. It regarded Lisa a moment, then swung its snout toward Rick.

"The hive has been expecting you," it announced.

"Our Regent has said that he finds your race most curious, and now I understand why. You are a little more like worms than I'd imagined, and indeed there is the stench of death about you."

The interior of the hive was greenhouse-hot, but the scientist's voice was cold and analytical. Rick, Rem, Kami, and Karen had been marched at gunpoint through the same entrance Rick had spied from the crater rim. There, their helmets and transpirators had been removed. One of the soldiers had carried Lisa in over his shoulder. She was still unconscious, groaning every so often in her delirium. Rick was being kept from her side. Kami, already succumbing to the hive's artificial atmosphere, had been shackled and dumped in a corner.

"That smell is the stink of your own soldiers' blood," Rick snarled at the scientist, gesturing to his green-smeared suit.

"The cornered creature's final attack," the Invid said to his white-robed group of barefoot assistants, in Tiresian for Rick's benefit. "The being uses words as weapons."

"What do you want with us? Why didn't your soldiers kill us?"

The scientist's snout sensors twitched, as if he was sniffing the air. "Perhaps we shall. But there is some information we require first. It would save us much bother if you'd simply agree to answer our questions—it might even save your lives."

Rick snorted. "Dream on, slug."

"As I thought," the scientist directed over his shoulder. He studied Rick a moment, then began to move down the line, pausing in front of Kami. "You were one of the Garudans selected by Tesla for the Regent's zoo, were you not?"

Kami leaned in as if to whisper something and snapped at the Invid's face, missing it by inches. Just as suddenly, a soldier threw a stranglehold on Kami from behind; in his weakened state, the Garudan was easily subdued.

The scientist shrugged it off and continued his appraisal of the group, *leering*, Rick thought, at Karen, and puzzling for a moment over Rem. "Why, you're *Tiresian*!" he said at last, and whirled through an excited turn to face his group. "We have a marvelous opportunity here to accomplish something invaluable for the realm. For the record," he added, looking to Rick, "where are the Robotech Masters?"

Rick beetled his brows. "The Masters?"

"Yes. Where is the Protoculture matrix?"

Rick groaned. *The thing had become a thorn in the galaxy's side.* "I don't know what you're talking about."

"That is hardly the response we require to justify sparing your lives, Earther. Be reasonable; you have Protoculture-fueled ships, Protoculture-based weapons . . . How did you come by these if not through contact with the Masters or the matrix? Unless, of course, the Flowers of Life grow on your homeworld . . ."

Rick fought to keep his surprise from registering. *So that's what they're after*, he thought, and recalled something Roy Fokker had told him almost ten years ago about the warning Lang had inadvertently keyed in the SDF-1 — Zor's warning about the Invid! *The Tirolian knew!—he knew the Invid would eventually go in search of the matrix!* Cabell's words to Lang rang in Rick's ears: *You must destroy the Invid here, destroy them while you still can!*

"I see something in your eyes, Human," the scientist was saying. "You know something."

Rick tightened his lips to a thin line.

"Then perhaps your dreams will tell us what we wish to know." The Invid waved a hand at the soldiers. "Take the Humans outside."

"You can't!" Kami bit out, his windpipe pinced in the soldier's grip. Others had stepped in to take hold of Rick, Karen, Rem, and Lisa. "They'll die!"

"Yes," the scientist said matter-of-factly, "they probably will."

CHAPTER
TEN

The psy scanners the Invid employed on Garuda (on Hunter and the rest) were patterned on similiar devices developed by the Tiresians. Ironically enough, the Robotech Masters had used the scanners on Zor shortly after his death, (and would use them again to monitor Zor Prime after the clone had been inserted into the Fifteenth ATAC), much as the Invid were using them on Rem.

History of the Second Robotech War, volume XXXI, "Tirol"

Dream a little dream with me.

Late twentieth-century song lyric

THE MALE HUMAN WAS DREAMING OF PURSUIT. HE WAS being chased by some sort of bird creature with an enormous wingspan, and—an Invid scientist had noted—a body shaped curiously like those of the raptorial birds depicted face-to-face on the Human's uniform insignia patch. The Human was running downhill, hopelessly out of control, with the bird pecking at his neck and back, flapping its great wings all the while. The backdrop for the dream was a world of ravaged landscapes, barren, cratered expanses of solidified volcanic flow. The Human was, and at the same time was not, both the pursued and pursuer. Crowds of other Humans seemed to be viewing the event from the sidelines, gesturing, pointing, applauding, laughing. One wore the face of the injured Human female who was presently being terrorized by dreams of her own—although she was sympathetic here, eager to help the running man, so it appeared.

"There's nothing of use to us in this one's thoughts," the head scientist said dismissively. Disappointed, he turned from the images in the instrumentality sphere and moved to the sphere his assistants had set up to monitor the dreams of the injured female.

Lisa, like Rick, Karen, and Rem, was strapped on her back to a kind of gurney, with her head positioned beneath a thick and heavy-looking ring-shaped device that resembled a scaled-down version of an MRI scanner. What the Invid scientists were calling dreams, however, were of the wide-eyed variety—altered states of consciousness, hellish ones by and large, normally kept locked away behind those proverbial doors of perception. Five minutes of exposure to Garuda's tainted atmosphere had been enough to elicit them. The scientists had no way of knowing whether this constituted what would amount to a lethal exposure—some Invid had lasted as long as half an hour without suffering irreversible effects. But these Humans were fragile things; physically strong for their size, it was true, but with limited tolerance for even the slightest of psychic assaults. They were inhabitants of the base realms, the sensate worlds at the lower end of the spectrum, as insubstantial as interstellar dust, and therefore highly expendable.

The leader of the white-robed group now activated the sphere attached to the device above Lisa's head, and here, too, the scientists encountered images of pursuit. Kami, muzzled and shackled in a corner of the hive's lab, was too deep into his own delirium to take note of their dismay.

"It seems to be something of a fixation with them," one of the assistants ventured.

The Human female was for all intents and purposes trapped on a spiral staircase that lacked any clear-cut terminus. Moreover, whatever it was that was pursuing her, hunting her, was so vague a thing as to be untranslatable by the sphere's Protoculture circuitry. There were momentary flashes of a feline creature, however, that brought to mind the Invid's own Hellcats. But the central concern of the dream and dreamer was the female's seemingly *reduced* size.

"Some reference to the Zentraedi, perhaps?"

The master scientist made a disgruntled sound. "Who can tell with these beings? Let us move on."

They grouped together in front of Karen's sphere next, arms folded and four-fingered hands tucked into the sleeves of their robes. The master among them had found himself strangely moved by this green-eyed, honey-haired Human; but unfortunately her dream-terrors proved to be as pedestrian and unrevealing as the previous ones. Her world was at least populated with a host of other beings, but they were there principally to insure that Karen was suitably horrified by the prospect of being buried alive.

The master expressed his distaste after a minute's viewing. "What a pitiful race . . . One wonders why they don't walk in fear of their own shadows. They've been more traumatized than Optera itself."

By now they had reached Rem—the Tiresian—and to their absolute astonishment, there in living color and as big as life in the center of the attendant sphere was *Optera*. This much could have been accounted for and dismissed, but next they found themselves viewing images of the Regis *in her pretransformed state*! And this was not the defoliated Optera of their ravenous present, but the edenic homeworld of their racial past—a verdant wonderland, with fields of Flowers basking in the warmth of the planet's twin suns, stretching as far as the eye could see across a landscape of arcadian beauty. Here was the lost harmony, the innocent splendor, the paradisiacal ease they could now access only in moments of collective trance, or at the mystical promptings of the Queen-Mother herself.

The scientists were reduced to silence, to tears of an ethereal sort.

"It's as if . . ."

"Say it," the master demanded.

". . . as if this one knew our world before the technovoyager's arrival."

"These are *his* thoughts."

With what would translate as shame, the master scientist deactivated the sphere and led his group to a sphere signifi-

cantly larger than the rest—their communications instrumentality, overshadowed by a relatively small specimen of
bubble-chambered brain.

"We must inform the Regent of this at once."

"And say what?"

"That we have found *Zor*!"

It had taken Jack all the inner strength he could muster
to keep from tearing down into that basin orchard with
guns blazing... He had heard the explosion that dropped
the first Scout ship, and had scrambled up to the top of the
crater rim like a mountain goat on amphetamines. Weapon
fire, follow-up blasts... by the time he got there, Rick and
the others were surrounded by Invid soldiers—more than
even he wanted to go up against. Lisa was down, Rick
bending over her. Kami, Rem, *Karen*! He had located a
safe vantage point and watched as his friends were led off
to the hive; then a short time later they had reappeared at
the dome's tunnellike entrance, this time stripped of their
transpirators. For some reason he had felt compelled to
time their exposure, sitting there powerless and near crazed
while the chronometer display counted off the minutes, *five
heart-stopping minutes*! He had run for the place where
they had stashed the cycs, found his way back to the trails
they had cut in predawn light, reentered the village... all
the while expecting Shock Troopers to emerge from the
ground, Hellcats or Robo-automata to leap on him from the
treetops. Pursued by nightmares...

Jack was just now finishing his hurried and breathless
recap, sitting cross-legged in the village longhouse and
sucking nutrient through a tube while the chief and some of
the Sentinels watched him.

"We've gotta spring them," he said at last, his thirst
slaked. "Right away, before they're moved."

The chief spoke to a member of the tribe; the male Garudan nodded his head a few times and took off in a rush.
"He has been instructed to pass the word," the chief explained. "We will be alerted if and when they are moved."

Learna was beside herself, her neck fur on end. She had

tried time and time again to Send herself to the hive, but each of her attempts had ended in failure. "Kami will die inside the hive. He must be returned to Garuda's air."

"He wasn't brought out with the rest of them," Jack told her, then turned to Cabell. "How long is too long?"

The old man made as if to stroke his beard under the suit. "I can't answer you, Jack. Tirol sent the Zentraedi here, the clones . . . I believe Rem and I are the first Tiresians to set foot on Garuda since Zor himself landed here."

"Can't you even estimate it?" Jack pressed him.

Cabell saw Jack's frustration and concern. "I don't imagine anything less than fifteen minutes would prove fatal." He was relieved to see Jack relax some.

"But why would they do that—why not just kill them, Wise One?" Gnea thought to ask.

The chief shrugged his powerful shoulders. "To torture them, perhaps to see if they could learn anything from their thoughts."

"All right," Max broke in, "suppose we wait till dusk. Your people will be heading back to the camps by then, right?"

Learna and the chief nodded, uncertain.

"We stage a diversionary raid on one of the other hives. Try to draw off as many of their mecha as we can. At the same time, a rescue team goes in."

"Agreed," Jack said, and some of the others joined him in voicing their support.

"I don't know," Cabell objected when everyone had quieted down. "It's risky. Those hives are much more complex than they appear."

"Well, of course it's risky," Jack argued, "but I don't see that we have any choice. What are we supposed to do—walk up and knock on the door? Uh, excuse me, but we were wondering if you might be willing to return our teammates—"

"There is an easier way to get them back."

Jack swung around to see who had interrupted him. When he saw it was Burak he fell silent, along with almost everyone else. The Perytonian had become something of an invisible being since the attempted mutiny, and to hear him suddenly speak, much less offer an opinion, was something of an event.

"You are forgetting our race in the hold," Burak said to the group's collective puzzlement.

"You mean 'ace in the hole,'" Jack corrected him.

"Whatever—"

"Tesla," Cabell exclaimed.

The devil from Peryton nodded.

"A hostage exchange?" Max asked.

Burak grinned beneath his mask. "Something like that."

On Optera, the Regent's servant reported only that five Sentinels had been captured on Garuda; he knew better than to steal the scientists' thunder. The Regent was relaxing in his sterile nutrient bath when the communique was received, having discovered that he could essentially guarantee messages merely by setting foot in the Olympic-size tub. Anxious for some news of Tesla, or information regarding the next destination of the Sentinels, he had spent the better part of a week in the bath, waiting. Now he practically ran to the throne room, sashing his robe as he approached the communicator sphere.

"Five Sentinels," he said out of breath. "Which ones?"

"A Garudan, three Humans, and . . . a Tiresian."

The Regent was pleased to learn that he had correctly anticipated the Sentinels' destination. He had passed the word to all his lieutenants that their troops be placed on alert. But it was captives he was after this time, not body counts, and no mention was to be made of his supposed assassination. With captives in hand, he hoped to learn whether or not Tesla had been acting alone, or in league with the rebels.

"A Tiresian you say."

"Yes, my liege. We have him here with us now."

The Regent peered at the terror-stricken face centered in the sphere's image, and brought his hand to his snout in a gesture of contemplation. "This one looks . . . familiar somehow."

"Well he should, Your Highness," the master scientist said as Rem's image de-rezzed. "We subjected the three Humans and the Tiresian to Garuda's atmosphere in an effort to extract the data you requested."

"And?" the Regent replied anxiously. "Did you discover the location of the Humans' homeworld—this *Earth*?"

"No. However, we may have a clue as to the whereabouts of the matrix," the scientist was quick to add. "My lord, allow us to screen for your pleasure the results of the Tiresian's exposure."

The Regent scowled at the sphere. "Do not bore me with details," he cautioned.

"You will find this anything but boring," the scientist told him.

The Regent viewed the playback for a moment, then staggered backward, collapsing into his high-backed throne. He sat agape, a defeated husband watching tapes of his wife . . . the seduction, the transgression, the cruel aftermath, all captured in graphic detail. That face, that face . . .

"How?" the Regent finally managed. "How is this possible? He is dead." *Or is he?* the Regent suddenly asked himself. Could he have been duped all these years into thinking Zor dead, when in fact . . . *No*, he thought. Zor was dead. But what then was the origin of these images? A simulagent, perhaps, like the very one he had created to take his place at the summit—

"We know Zor is dead," the scientist was saying. "But somehow his memory lives on in this one—a clone, we suspect."

The Regent came bolt upright in the chair. "The matrix!"

"Precisely."

"He must be sent to Optera at once!"

The scientist inclined his head some. "Of course, my lord. But would it not be best to take advantage of Garuda's proximity to Haydon IV? May I remind Your Highness of the devices there that are far superior—"

"Yes, yes. See that it is arranged. I will leave immediately," the Regent added, already on his feet.

"There is one small detail, however..."

"What?"

"We have learned that the Regis is there."

"On Haydon IV?!"

"Yes, my lord. Should we wait until she leaves before transporting the clone?"

The Regent started to agree, but bit off his words. *Why not let her see the clone?* he asked himself. *Why not let her look once more upon Zor's face, into his very thoughts and recollections?* He laughed out loud. *To be there, to see her face when the clone was presented...*

"No, you are not to wait," the Regent said shortly. "In fact, you are simply to say that you have a *gift* for her—a gift from her *loving husband*!"

"I need to see Tesla at once," Burak told Janice as he stepped from the shuttle's ramp into the SDF-7's docking bay. Gnea and Max had ridden up with him, but they were already rushing off to meet with Wolff and Vince Grant.

Janice thought she heard something akin to arrogance in the Perytonian's voice, but decided to leave it unchallenged. "Of course, Burak," she said, motioning for him to follow her.

They didn't speak for the duration of the long walk to the cargo hold that had become Tesla's quarters; but short of the closed hatch Burak stopped and said, "Alone." The Perytonian positioned himself between Janice and the hatch.

"Something I should know?" she risked.

"You should know that he doesn't like you very much," Burak whispered back menacingly, gesturing over one shoulder with his two-thumbed hand.

Janice laughed. "And we make such an adorable couple. Is it my looks or my personality?"

Burak contorted his demon face for her benefit.

"Keep doing that and your face is going to stay that way," she said, moving off.

Burak snorted and entered the hold, pulling smuggled

Fruits from his uniform and casually tossing them to Tesla, who was seated on an enormous crate.

"What's this all about?" the Invid asked peevishly, as one of the mutant Fruits bounced off his snout.

"I have good news," Burak announced, assuming a proud stance and allowing Tesla to regard him a moment. "You claim to be more evolved than the Regent. That means the scientists would recognize your greatness, does it not?"

Tesla ducked his snout, looked around the hold like a felon, and motioned for Burak to keep his voice down. "Yes, certainly," he said. "But what does this have to do with anything?"

Burak studied one of the Fruits. "Suppose I could arrange for an audience with the scientists here?"

Tesla shot to his feet, horrified by the prospect. "You must—"

"Hunter and a few of the others were captured," Burak quickly explained, gazing up at the Invid. "I suggested that we exchange you for them. That way—"

"*You what?*"

"That way you'll be able to assert your right to the throne—just as you . . . wanted . . . What's wrong?"

Wearily, Tesla had reseated himself. "You fool," he muttered, shaking his hands. "You've just sealed my fate."

"B-but . . ."

"It's too soon, Burak, too soon. The Regis will send me to the pits." He glanced up. "The next time you see Tesla he'll be a maggot."

Burak made a distressed sound, seeing his own dreams for Peryton go up in smoke; and just then Janice, Vince Grant, Gnea, and Lron burst into the hold. The amazon Praxian had an armed blaster in her hands.

"Everybody ready?" Janice said brightly, looking back and forth between Burak and Tesla. Cautiously, Lron and Grant had moved in to shackle the Invid's wrists and place a prisoner bib around his neck.

"All right, Invid, let's go," Gnea said, brandishing the weapon.

Lron gave Tesla a light shove.

Tesla looked down and caught Janice's smile.

"Guess this is your lucky day," she told him.

Jonathan Wolff sat on the bridge of the cruiser with his feet up on one of the duty-station consoles. He was alone for a change, Grant and most of the crew having rushed off for the ordnance bay. Well within reach, on the floor beside the command chair, was a bottle of Southlands brandy. It was almost empty.

"To rescues," Wolff said now, toasting Garuda through the forward viewport and lifting the bottle to his lips. He gulped down half an inch and shuddered.

The Hunters had gone and gotten themselves captured, along with Karen, Rem, and that Garudan—Kami. And Max or somebody figured they could swap them for Tesla, only Wolff didn't put much stock in it. Of course he hadn't said that to them—oh no, mustn't burst anyone's bubble, chin up and all that ancient rot. But that was what he *felt*. The Invid would go back on their word, maybe the Sentinels would go back on theirs, somebody would betray somebody else . . . he didn't need to be there to see it all go down.

"So here's to betrayals," he said, and took another pull. "Minmei, you . . . *meanie*."

Doubled over in laughter, Wolff swung his legs off the control panel. Yes, she was a *meanie* all right, telling him to take a walk, falling in love with his enemy. "*Earth's* enemy," Wolff emphasized. "Have to give the man his due." He drank again, staring blankly at the bottle when he lowered it, rocking back and forth.

Without warning, a tone sounded on the bridge and nearly sent him out of his skin. He reached out for the com stud and slammed his fist down, missing it, but getting it on the third try.

"Wolff," he said.

"A small craft," one of the new crewmen reported. "Not much bigger than an Alpha. Transport, maybe."

"Put it up," Wolff said, swinging to a monitor screen.

"No can do, sir. Too far for visuals."

"Is it within range?"

"Just barely."

"Armed?"

"Negative, sir. But it launched from the sector where the Hunters are being held."

Wolff contemplated the blip on the screen.

"Let it go," he said. "The way things stand, what difference is one small ship going to make?"

CHAPTER
ELEVEN

Unlike the Zentraedi, who had in a sense taught them every-thing they knew about warfare, the Invid were not above the idea of taking hostages. The reason for this can be traced back to the chaotic period following the defoliation of Optera by the Masters' newly created clone warriors. The Regent was convinced that Zor had stolen the Flowers of Life merely to offer them up in exchange for the Regis herself. Emulating the Tiresian then, the Regent had sent out his new army not to kill, but to capture Zor, in the hopes of holding him hostage for the return of the Flowers!

Bloom Nesterfig, *The Social Organization of the Invid*

"**I** JUST THINK WE SHOULD TALK THIS OVER FIRST, that's all," Tesla told the assembled Sentinels, Bioroid pilots, and assorted members of Kami's tribe.

He could see that the Garudans weren't exactly thrilled to have an Invid in their midst—particularly the Invid who had supervised the Regent's specimen mission some time ago—and he was beginning to wonder whether he would even make it out of the village alive, let alone into one of the farm-hives. Still, he reasoned, if he could come up with a better plan than the hostage exchange the Sentinels seemed to be favoring at the moment, he might be able to save himself from either fate.

"After all," Tesla continued, undaunted, "it doesn't sound to me like you have this thing entirely worked out. The whens, the wheres, the hows . . . And for all I know, the Regent may have given orders for me to be shot on sight."

This much was true, and as a result the group lapsed into an uneasy silence. They couldn't simply *call* the farm, nor could they just waltz in waving the proverbial white flag. But this was where Tesla was supposed to supply answers; and instead he was suddenly acting as though he couldn't bear to part company with his captors. In private Janice had told everyone to expect as much, although she had been vague about the reasons.

"Then what the heck have we been keeping you around for all this time?" Jack shouted. "You're supposed to be our ace in the hole, not some hunk of dead weight."

"Jack, I'm hurt, I'm really hurt," Tesla returned, trying to put emotion behind the words.

The shuttle was back on the planet's surface now. Vince Grant was still aboard the SDF-7; but almost everyone else with the exception of Teal had shuttled down. Jean's team was in the process of erecting an atmosphere-controlled geodesic medical module on the outskirts of the village to house Rick and the others once they were freed. Veidt and Sarna had affirmed that five or even fifteen minutes' exposure to Garuda's atmosphere wouldn't prove lethal; but at the same time the danger to Rick and the others was increasing with each moment they were kept from proper treatment. Just what constituted "proper" treatment had yet to be determined; and Veidt refused to speculate until the Humans were rescued and run through a battery of tests.

Burak was sorry he had opened his mouth, but there was nothing he could do to change things. Besides, Tesla was giving it his best shot and might yet convince the Sentinels to adopt a different course of action.

"Let's hear it, if you've got a better plan," Miriya Sterling was saying.

Tesla put his hands behind his back and paced back and forth, the crown of his head inches from the longhouse rafters. The breathing gear the med group had fashioned for the Invid was a jury-rigged affair of masks, tanks, and tubes, giving Tesla a decidedly elephantine appearance.

"How's this?" he asked at last, swinging around to face

Jack, Cabell, the chief, and a few others. "Divert attention away from the farm by initiating a raid—"

"We're one step ahead of you, Tesla," Max said, interrupting. "Infiltrate a small party at the same time, and end up giving your troops more hostages."

"It doesn't have to end that way," Tesla argued. "Not if I'm with the commando team."

Jack grunted. "What do you know that Rick didn't know? We went in quiet as mice and they nailed us."

"It was the mecha—your Hovercycles—that gave you away. The farm's defenses can sense Protoculture activity. So even though you got past the Inorganics . . ."

Tesla left the sentence unfinished, pleased to see that the Sentinels were offering one another surprised glances.

"No wonder they got the jump on us," Jack remarked.

"What about weapons, Tesla?" Cabell thought to ask.

"Weapons, too," the Invid answered him.

Max looked around the longhouse. "Where does that leave us?"

"Swords, crossbows, spears," Gnea said proudly.

Cabell shook his head. "They're no use against Inorganics."

"Grenades, then," Learna chimed in. "Rocket launchers—"

"And these," said the chief, as two of his tribesmen dragged an odd-looking crate into the hut.

Inside were a dozen Karbarran firearms not unlike Lron's own small-bore. Each wooden and metal-fitted rifle had a large globular fixture forward of the trigger guard and forestock lever. "We received many such crates during the final days of the Masters' empire," the chief went on to explain as Lron hefted one of the weapons.

"Yes," Lron said, "Karbarra was exporting rebellion then." He glanced over at Tesla. "Until the Invid appeared."

Max, too, was studying the Invid. "All right, Tesla," he said, coming to his feet. "We'll play this one your way. But all deals are off at the first sign of any monkey business."

Tesla regarded Max and the others through his hastily fashioned mask. "Now, why would I want to do that when I've had enough trouble just trying to act *Human*?"

This time the team was principally XT—Lron and Crysta, Gnea and Bela, with Learna as guide. That Jack would accompany them had been taken for granted; and, after Tesla's plan had been given the okay, Janice signed on. The Praxians felt more comfortable with their one-handed crossbows, shields, and shortswords than anything else the Sentinels could offer in the way of weaponry, and Gnea wouldn't part company with her spearlike *naginata*. But the others carried Karbarran air rifles, satchels of command-detonated explosives, conventional fragmentation grenades, and rocket launchers. Shortly after Garuda's midnight, the eight-member team was inserted by Garudan flitters to within twenty miles of the crater, allowing them ample time to reach the farm-hive before sunrise.

At the same time, Wolff and the Sterlings met back at the shuttle to coordinate plans for their joint diversionary raid against two neighboring farms. It was decided that the Veritechs and Hovertanks would commence their strikes at sunrise, when the Garudan slaves would still be in the camps.

"We're going to concentrate our fire against the orchards, here and here," Max briefed his squadron later on, pointing to areas on the maps Learna had provided. The hives themselves—processing plants really—were almost certainly protected by energy shields like the one the Invid had thrown over Tiresia's Royal Hall during the battle for Tirol. But since the Sentinels' main objective was to draw out the enemy mecha, Max saw no reason why targeting the precious Optera tree plantations couldn't achieve the same result.

"Colonel Wolff's tankers will position themselves along this ridgeline and move in after you've completed your initial runs. Then you're to pulverize that hive. If we dump enough into that shield we might be able to punch through." Similar all-out bursts had worked against the Karbarran hives. Max scanned his small audience. "Any questions?" When all the headshaking was over, he added, "All right then, let's saddle up."

Outside the shuttle, he caught sight of Miriya, who had been off briefing the Skull's Red contingent, and hurried over to her just as she was scampering up into the Alpha's cockpit. She had seemed preoccupied during the meeting with Wolff, and absent even now when he asked her if everything was all right.

"Yeah, fine," she said, offering him a weak smile beneath her transpirator.

"You don't look fine," he told her, touching her hair. "Maybe you should sit this one out." She laughed at the suggestion, more out of surprise, he suspected, than anything else. A former Quadrono sit out a fight?

"Max, I'm just a little tired." She donned the thinking cap, climbed the notch ladder, and settled herself in the cockpit seat. "Now wipe that concerned look off your face," she told him before lowering the canopy.

He forced a smile her way, readjusted his mask, and ran to his own mecha. In five minutes both squadron teams were up, tearing through Garuda's crimson predawn skies.

The farms they had chosen to hit were some fifty miles southwest of the crater farm, surrounded by extensive forests of Optera trees, which from Max's point of view resembled outsized melon patches; the hive itself was a freeze-frame shot of a hydrogen bomb's first-stage canopy.

He took hold of the stick and ordered the Skull to follow him in, loosing a dozen napalm torpedoes from the Alpha's undercarriage pylons at treetop-level. Angry plumes of liquid fire fountained above the ground fog behind him as the VT went ballistic; Max turned to look over his shoulder as the rest of the squadron dove in for their runs, each explosion spreading dollops of burning stuff from tree to tree. Skull One rolled over and went in again, incinerating a patch of forest west of the hive now, while Miriya's team gave the east quadrant hell. Then all at once there were Invid Shock Troopers in the air, rising out of the leaping flames and black smoke like a swarm of angry hornets.

"We've got company, Skull Leader," one of Max's wingmen reported. "Multiple signals at eight o'clock."

Max turned his attention from the ascending mecha and twisted around to his right: twenty or more Pincer Ships were approaching from the direction of the crater farm.

"Coming around to zero one zero," Max said into the tac net. "Help me engage, Blue Danube."

"On my way, Skull One. Rolling out . . ."

Max went for missile lock on the lead Pincer and thumbed off two heat-seekers; they found the ship as it climbed, quartering it and a second Pincer in the process. But the Invid were answering the challenge, and Max was forced to break high and right as streams of annihilation disks screamed into the pocket he had vacated. His wingmen split and boostered out in the nick of time, chased by clusters of Shock Troopers from the Invid's counteroffensive group.

Max imaged the Alpha over to Battloid mode at the top of his climb, targeting data scrolling across his display screens now, and the net a tangle of requests and mad shrieks. A hail of missiles tore from the VT's open shoulder racks and dropped into the midst of the Invid pursuit group, wiping out five of their number. Max went to guns with the remaining two, hands clenching the HOTAS, trapshooting the Invid with the Alpha's rifle/cannon as they streaked by him.

Elsewhere in the field, Miriya's team was holding its own against the mecha born in that inferno below. Half the trees were on fire now, thick smoke roiling in Garuda's dawn, while Humans and Invid exchanged salvos of death. Battloids and Troopers grappled gauntlet to claw.

"Guess we succeeded in getting their attention," Max said to no one in particular. He chinned Miriya's frequency and asked for an update; he repeated the request when she didn't respond, then reconfigured his ship and dropped down to have a look for himself.

Miriya had gone to Battloid and was executing her own

version of a Fokker Feint when Max caught up with her. There were four Shock Troopers hovering around her mecha, pulling sting-and-runs. He smiled as he watched her ace one of them with the autocannon; but that look collapsed when he realized how slow she was to react to follow-up energy Frisbees delivered by the remainder of the group. Max was close enough now to throw himself into the fight; but the sight of her sloppiness had left him shaken, and he almost got himself dusted.

"Miriya, what's wrong?" he said when the last of the four had been dispatched. "Miriya!"

"I . . . don't know, Max," she answered him after a moment. "Dizzy spell."

"I want you to return to base."

Miriya's face came up on Skull One's commo screen. "I'll be all right. It's better now."

"Forget it—"

"Max!" Wolff's voice suddenly boomed through the net. "We've got troubles! Inorganics—hundreds of them!"

Max looked away from Miriya's image and chinned the com freak. "Your Pack should be able to handle those things, Wolff," he said.

"It's not us they're after, Commander," Wolff said, just as gruffly. "The sons of bitches have turned them loose on the camp—they're attacking the Garudans!"

A short distance from the besieged orchard, Wolff's Hovertank team was well into the forests surrounding the second farm. From the ridgeline above the dome-shaped hive, where the Pack had been Guardian-configured, Wolff had been able to observe the Skull's fiery treetop passes. He had then given the order for his tankers to open fire. They hadn't lobbed five minutes' worth of projectiles into the forest when the first wave of Inorganics had appeared —Hellcats, galloping across Garuda's tundra and heading straight for the ridge. They were followed a minute later by ranks of the bipedal demonic-looking Robo-trolls known as Cranns and Odeons.

Wolff had hated the things ever since he went up against

them on Tirol, and had been looking forward to engaging them—anything to get Minmei off his mind for a while, to keep his hand from reaching out for a bottle . . . So he had ordered the Pack over to standard mode and led the charge down the rocky slope, only to find that the Inorganics had changed course. And it had only taken a moment to figure out the reason behind the tactic: the Invid were planning to use the Garudans as the Sentinels had the Invid's life-giving trees—for *diversion*! The XT labor force was strung out for more than a mile along a sparsely wooded hillside guarded by a company of armed and weapon-wielding Invid soldiers. It was then that Wolff had opened the net to Max.

The Skull fighters were overhead now; Wolff could see them through breaks in the trees' clustered, billiard-ball canopies. Shock Troopers and Pincer Ships were right on their tails.

Wolff's Hovertanks broke out of the forest a moment after Skull One Touched down; the Alpha was in Guardian mode, with the rifle/cannon gripped in one gauntlet, stammering its harsh greeting to the Hellcats. Dozens of Inorganics burst apart as armor-piercing rounds ripped into the pack, but five times that number made it through the VT's still-forming line, bounding over the mecha and continuing their mad rush for the Garudans. Aware of the situation now, the helpless slaves had broken ranks and were attempting to flee; most of them were cut down instantly by bursts from the soldiers' forearm guns, while others fell to the first wave of Inorganics, torn apart by Hellcats or roasted by bolts from the Cranns' orifice-dimpled weapons spheres.

Wolff ordered the Pack to spread out and form a second line; the Hovertanks reconfigured and began to fire at will, decimating much of the second sortie wave, but suddenly forced to deal with the Shock Troopers as well. Annihilation disks stormed into the tankers' midst, tearing up the land and overturning two of the mecha. Wolff could see that members of Max's blue team were going over to Batt-loid and repositioning themselves opposite the Pack to form the second leg of a V formation. Wolff called for a cannonade as the Inorganics rushed into the notch. Pounded with explosive rounds the tundra shook and bellowed; the ridge trapped the concussive sounds and hurled them back, as Inorganics and Shock Troopers alike were reduced to gobs of white-hot metal, geysers of fire in the already superheated air.

Miriya's Red team came in just then to add their deafening movement to the score. Pincer Ships and VTs went face-to-face, hammering away at one another, while missiles and projectiles corkscrewed through the firestorm and smoke.

Wolff told his B team to hold their ground; at the same time he and the other A tankers battled their way over scorched terrain and through flaming stands of trees toward the Garudans' march of death. Prevented from ascending the hillside by rows of Invid soldiers and vulnerable below to the Inorganics' unchecked advance, the vulpine XTs were being slaughtered. Wolff thought he could hear their wailing clear through the tank's canopy and the tac net's cacophony of calls. The Pack couldn't fire for fear of killing even more of them; so instead Wolff led the tankers on a flat-out collision course straight to where the Inorganics had become bunched up at the base of the hill. The tanks smashed their way into the thick of the slaughter, downswept deflection bows cutting Cranns and Odeons in half. Hellcats leaped on the hovering mecha, only to be blasted to smithereens by in-close guns, or crushed by hand when some of the Pack reconfigured to Battloid mode.

Meanwhile, at the edge of the forest Max's VT teams were getting the upper hand. Pincer and Shock Trooper ships were falling out of the sky like ducks on a bad day at the marsh. Miriya's Reds accounted for most of those kills; Wolff could just discern them overhead, flying circles around the enemy pilots. He caught sight of one VT in particular as it was completing some sort of aerial pirouette that had left three Pincers in ruin; he was thinking that it must have been Miriya's, until he saw the VT sustain a shot any cadet could have dodged. Wolff watched it plummet toward a ravaged area of woodland.

"That's the place they got jumped," Jack said, pointing out a damaged row of Optera trees at the bottom of the slope. The hulks of the three Scout ships had been removed, but there was evidence of the fires the explosions had touched off. "Then they were dragged into the hive." Jack handed binoculars up to Lron, once again indicating the direction. "You can just make out the entrance or whatever it is."

Tesla gave him the Invid word for the portal, mumbling something Jack found unintelligible.

"Like I said: whatever it is."

Careful not to disturb his transpirator, Lron took a look through the armored glasses and passed them along to Crysta. She was upping the intensity some, when Learna's trill-like signal reached them from somewhere in the trees. A moment later, the Garudan appeared at the base of the slope, motioning the team down. Gnea and Bela were crouched behind her, masked and vigilant, looking more than ever like barbaric gladiators lifted from some Roman arena. Jack tapped Janice on the shoulder and got everyone under way.

They had reached the crater well before dawn, without incident despite the presence of stepped-up Inorganic patrol teams. Not just Hellcats, but Cranns and Odeons—bizarre enough creatures by daylight, and positively frightening in the predawn ground fog. Even these hadn't deterred the free Garudans from putting in an appearance, though; only this time it was more than curiosity that motivated them: many had armed themselves with Karbarran air rifles, hoisting them in a display of support as the team passed. Just before sunrise at the crater rim, Jack had seen flashes of explosive light in the southwestern skies, rolls of distant thunder—the Skull's bombing run against the neighboring farm. Shortly thereafter, scores of Shock Troopers had risen from the basin and flown toward the sound of the guns.

"Any activity?" Jack asked when he reached the base of the slope.

"Nothing so far," Learna told him. "We went as far as the hive."

Jack turned to Tesla. "What do you think?" he said angrily. He had no patience left for the Invid's malingering. Keeping Tesla concealed on the trail had led to more than a few hairy moments; and on the slope he had behaved less like a sentient creature than an out-of-control boulder. But now the time had come for Tesla to earn his keep. "What's their routine?"

Tesla glanced at what could be seen of the hive through the trees. "Difficult to say, what with all the activity you've stirred up. Normally, the slaves would be arriving any minute now." Tesla looked up at one of the trees' vine-encrusted globe canopies. "Pity, too," he mused. "All this ripe fruit going to waste.

Jack brandished a long-bladed dirk as Tesla reached out to pluck a particularly succulent-looking piece. "You haven't earned it yet, Tesla. Besides, you don't really want to take off the mask, do you?"

Tesla thought it over. There was no reason he couldn't lift the mask for the time it would take to gobble down some fruit; but he decided not to bother arguing the point. So he simply left the fruit to rot instead of adding it to the samples he had already stuffed into the pockets of his robes.

"No, I suppose not," he said after a moment.

Jack ordered him to take the point; and in ten minutes the team arrived at the hive's entrance. It was faintly lit, a half-moon−shaped tunnel twenty-five-feet high and composed of what looked like solidified sea foam. There seemed to be a slight shimmering to the air inside, but this ceased when Tesla identified himself to the scanner. A voiceprint, Jack thought, but he couldn't be sure.

The tunnel was deadly hot, evil-smelling even through

the masks' filters, and reminded Jack of fiber-optic vids he had seen of the human body's arterial system. It terminated in a rotunda, whose enormity and crepuscular illumination Jack found disorienting. Dozens of corridors emptied into the area, like detonator horns on an old-fashioned naval mine.

"We can dispense with these contraptions," Tesla was saying, pulling the transpirator from his snout. He took a deep breath and smiled at everyone. Jack could see that he was taking obvious delight in their amazement.

"This is our foyer," Tesla said, with an elaborate wave of his arm.

Jack checked the display on the biosensor Jean had strapped on his wrist. Satisfied, he slipped the filtration mask from his mouth, determined to keep a straight face. Still wary, he sniffed at the air, found it slightly dank but breathable, and gave the all-clear for the others to follow his example. "Which way?" he demanded, leading with his chin.

Tesla pointed to the circular shaft directly overhead. "There." With a theatrical gesture, he motioned the team to gather round him. No sooner had they done so than they found themselves imprisoned by some sort of tractor beam that was lifting them en masse toward the overhead shaft. Gnea brought the tip of her lance to the ribbed underside of Tesla's neck.

"No," he told her, up on tiptoes to ease the contact. "You have it all wrong. This is simply our . . . elevator system."

Jack and Janice were down in a combat crouch, weapons drawn, searching the beam's translucent circumference for any sign of danger. Lron, Crysta, Bela, and Kami were similarly postured, Karbarran air rifles at high port, crossbows armed. Tesla continued to protest for the duration of the thirty-second ascent into the dome's upper reaches.

Slowly, the tractor field began to de-rezz.

Jack had relaxed some by the time the beam shut down;

hen all at once he saw four Invid sentries swinging around
o face them, forearm cannons raised.

Max had seen Miriya's Alpha go down. He had his own
VT in Battloid mode now, and was running it toward the
rash site through a section of burning forest. Two of his
eam were dead; at least that many of Miriya's had died as
vell. He wasn't sure how Wolff was doing, but he had
een more than one Hovertank overturned by Shock
Trooper anni disks. Max didn't even want to think about
he Garudan slaves. And suddenly there was Miriya to
vorry about.

The mecha's scanners caught sight of something up
head, and Max called for increased intensity, studying the
iosensor data displays. A minute later he had visuals. It
vas Miriya's Red Alpha alright, in lopsided Guardian con-
iguration, radome tipped to the ground—a wounded bird.

Then Max spotted the Hellcats—four of them, attack-
ng the VT's canopy with a frenzy, battering it with down-
vard blows of their armored heads. He could see that one
norganic had managed to get a claw inside, and was wav-
ng it around, presumably hoping to slice Miriya to shreds.
The four turned at the same moment to show Max their
leaming fangs and sword-edged shoulder horns; two hunt-
nates leaped for the VT straightaway, but he already had
he rifle/cannon locked on them. They came apart in midair
ike clay pigeons. Max holed a third where it stood glaring
t him, and now the final 'Cat snatched its paw from the
unctured canopy, reared up, and came at him. Max tried
o sidestep the Battloid when the Hellcat jumped, but his
iming was off; the Inorganic latched on to the mecha's
blative head shields and began to ram its snout against the
ermaplas visor. Reflexively, Max pressed himself back
nto the cockpit seat; he had a larger-than-life view of the
razed thing's snapping mouth and false gullet. The 'Cat
vas snarling, trying desperately to slice open the Battloid's
elly with the churning motion of its razor-sharp hind
laws. Max shut down the external pickups and armed the
ead lasers. The angle was almost too oblique, but the

Hellcat's back was heaving in and out of the targetin
brackets and Max thought he might have a chance. H
raised the Battloid's left arm, gripped the 'Cat around th
waist, and tugged it into the lasers' field. Then he triggere
the in-close guns. The Inorganic brought its head up as th
light beams seared into its backside; it took Max's follow
up pulse right through the eyes and dropped to the ground
lifeless.

Max stomped the thing twice. He imaged over t
Guardian mode and pulled his mask tight as he popped th
mecha's canopy. Miriya had yet to show herself. Scamper
ing up along the Red's downswept wing, he peered into th
shattered cockpit and began to fumble with the manua
release levers.

"Miriya!"

He called her name twice more before he succeeded i
springing the ship's protective blister. She appeared ur
harmed, but unconscious. More troubling, however, wa
the fact that the Hellcat had ripped off her mask; she ha
been breathing Garuda's atmosphere for a dangerously lon
time.

CHAPTER
TWELVE

*Several commentators have felt compelled to point out that
Jonathan's Wolff's "slip" [sic: see Mizner's Rakes and Rogues;
The True Story of the SDF-3 Expeditionary Mission] was perhaps
the pivotal event of the Third Robotech War. The reasoning goes
something like this: If Wolff had fired on the Invid ship, Rem would
never had reached Haydon IV; and without Rem, the Regis would
not have been as likely to instruct her Sensor Nebulae to search
the Galaxy's outermost arms for evidence of the matrix, and would
not, therefore, have found Earth until years after the Expeditionary mission returned. The reader must decide for him or herself
whether anything is to be gained by such speculation; but I would
point out that [Mizner's] reasoning can be made to apply in both
directions. It is as easy to blame Lynn-Minmei as it is Jonathan
Wolff.*

Footnote in Zens Bellow's *The Road to Reflex Point*

AN INVID SHIP, A SMALL SHUTTLE, HAD DOCKED AT
Haydon IV's spaceport facility. The Regis had been told
that it was from Garuda—and bearing gifts.

She was in her temporary headquarters high atop one of
the city's ultratech architectural wonders when news of the
ship's arrival was delivered to her. *Out of reach,* she liked
to think; distanced from the cold, unsettling presence of the
planet's armless, hovering creatures, the displaced and still
discontent Praxian Sisterhood, her own discomforting
discoveries . . . And out of the Regent's reach, his dark
schemes and mad plans.

But if anything, Haydon IV had only compounded the
misery she had carried here from Optera and Praxis. She
felt at the mercy of a confused longing she could not de-
fine; a need to break free of this horizonless condition.

She supposed that she should have been grateful that
Haydon IV's inhabitants hadn't in any way trifled with her

or denied her anything; but neither had they accepted her as the evolved being she fancied herself to be. It was more accurate to say they had *tolerated* her presence—as if they were all privy to some grand arcane mystery she couldn't even discern, much less unravel. And furthermore she sensed that this had something to do with the world's equally mysterious founder/creator—Haydon. The data-banks she had searched for answers to her own evolutionary puzzles gave some glimpse into his life, but hardly enough to form a complete portrait of the being. And she confessed to a certain trepidation at expanding her efforts along these lines. Already the very foundation of her own life's work had been shaken by what she had uncovered in Haydon's transphysical musings, and all at once she felt too unsure of herself and her ambitions to permit much more in the way of contradiction. There were hints, though, that she was not, as she had imagined, *in control of things*; that the theft of the Flowers, the Invid's quest, even Zor's misdeeds, were but part of a much grander design—one in which she, too, did little more than play out a role. And that role . . . that role demanded she accept that what she sought was not the Flowers of Life, but the stuff that had been conjured from them by Zor himself—the *Protoculture*!

As she saw it—as she wanted to see it—Protoculture was a malicious energy, a malignancy that did nothing but fuel the war machine of the Masters and her deluded ex-husband. To see it as more would be to admit she had been wrong after all, that the Regent's course was the truer one, the predestined one.

And suddenly he had sent her some sort of gift.

She was pacing the floor like a caged beast now, waiting for the unsolicited thing to be brought up to her. Finally, two of her husband's "scientists" were admitted to her quarters; she recognized one of them as a master she had herself evolved for the express purpose of overseeing Flower gathering on Garuda—another of the cursed worlds Zor had for some reason seen fit to cultivate.

"Your Grace," the scientist directed up to her, bowing.

"The Regent regrets that he could not be here in person to bestow his gift."

The Regis made a scoffing sound. "If he had come in person, I wouldn't be here to receive him. Now, have the thing brought in and take your leave, *underling*."

"Of course, Your Worship," the scientist said, bowing once more. "Only it is not so much a 'thing' . . ."

"What then?" she asked him, arms akimbo.

"More in the way of a live presentation—but one that will surely prove most enlightening." The scientist shouted a few quick commands over his shoulder, and two Invid soldiers marched into the room. Sandwiched between them was a small Tiresioid male, narcotized, so it appeared.

Puzzled, the Regis reduced her stature some to get a better look at him. One of the soldiers tilted the Tiresioid's face up for her inspection.

It was Zor.

A tight scream worked its way up from the very depths of her being, and she came close to losing consciousness, falling back from the soldiers and their terrible trophy and crashing against a communicator sphere.

"A clone, Your Grace, a *clone*!" the scientist was shouting, aware of the Regis's distress. "We meant you no ill."

"How dare you!" she bellowed, frightfully enough to send both soldiers and scientists to their knees, and Rem facefirst to the floor.

"We subjected the clone to the Garudan atmosphere and discovered that his dreams spoke of things we were certain you would find—"

"Silence!" the Regis said, cutting off the scientist's rush of words. "I know what you *thought*," she added, more composed now. "And I know what the Regent meant by sending me this . . . *clone*. On your feet!"

Hesitantly, the four Invid did as instructed, leaving Rem where he lay. "Your Highness," the master scientist began on a sheepish note, "Haydon IV's devices will permit us to gaze even deeper into the clone's cellular memory. Perhaps some clue regarding the Masters or the missing Protoculture matrix . . ."

"Yes," she answered him, looking down at Rem as he groaned and rolled over. It took all her strength to keep from reaching out to touch him. Would he remember her? she wondered. Would the clone's cellular memory reveal what Zor had been thinking when he seduced her, when he returned to Optera for the seedlings, backed by an army of warrior giants? Would that same memory reveal the path the matrix had taken, the course she would follow? . . . "Conduct your experiments," she told the relieved group. "Show me the future of our race!"

Jonathan Wolff was beyond believing in miracles, but he was hard-pressed for a better word to describe the sight of several hundred Garudans charging onto the scene to rescue their enslaved brethren. They were cresting the hill-top now—armed with everything from war clubs and bolos and grapnel-shaped things to Karbarran air weapons and antimecha rockets—and dropping down on the Invid soldiers who were keeping the slaves hemmed in. A dozen or so Bioroids on Hoverplatforms were providing them with air support, employing their stem-mounted cannons to rain destruction on Hellcats and Cranns alike.

Countless defenseless Garudans had been killed in the Inorganics' genocidal attack, but that didn't stop the survivors from rallying once they realized that their world had committed itself to an all-or-nothing stand. They rushed the Invid lines, which were already strained to the breaking point, and fell upon the offworlders with a violence only blind fury could release. It took five, ten, often fifteen Garudans to bring down a single armored soldier, but one by one the enemy fell. Some were pummeled to death, others disintegrated by their own weapons, and still others were stripped of their masks and respirator tanks and left to run amok, crazed long before the spores could work their effect—crazed by the naked fear of that end.

Spurred on by this reversal, the Wolff Pack and Skull Squadron pulled out all the stops. Until this moment, con-cern for the well-being of Rick and their other captured comrades had to some extent weakened their resolve; and it

took the Garudans' desperate charge to make them remember what the fight for liberation was all about. Re-
inspired, VT pilots and Hovertankers let loose their own
shadow selves, and swept like avenging angels through
ruptured sky and forests infernal. Shock Troopers, soldiers,
Optera trees, the farms themselves—nothing was to be
spared their wrath.

With total abandon, Wolff urged his mecha deeper and
deeper into the madness, destroying, crippling, killing. For
one instant he rejoiced at hearing Miriya Sterling's voice
over the tac net—she was presently riding tandem in
Max's Alpha/Beta fighter—but that was no more than a
fleeting reminder of a past life. He considered himself one
of the dead now, in no world's hell but his own. And from
that hollow center came a murderous intent that knew no
bounds. He could only hope that some of the Sentinels
would live to see victory that day.

"Behind you!" Janice shouted.

But Jack had already seen them and was halfway
through his turn, the rocket launcher atop his shoulder.
Three Invid soldiers were advancing up the corridor, their
forearm cannons booming. Jack triggered his shot and
caught one of the XTs dead center. The explosion was
enough to drop the other two, but only momentarily; they
were back on their feet in an instant, resuming their advance while Jack reached for the grenades clipped to his
web belt.

"We've got them!" he heard Lron, or possibly Crysta,
growl. The Karbarrans were positioned on either side of
the corridor terminus, grenades in their outstretched mitts.
"Now!" Lron said, and the two pivoted and released.

Jack flattened himself against the floor and covered his
head; the roar and concussive heat washed over him and he
rolled to one side, running through a quick check of everyone's position. Janice was behind him, kneeling over the
quivering mass that was Tesla; Gnea and Bela were off to
the right, along a section of curved, featureless wall just
short of a second corridor terminus. Learna was opposite

them, near the tubestand and sphere arrangement Tesla had called a communicator. The four Invid soldiers who had greeted them after the "elevator" ride were sprawled on the floor, dead; two with arrows sunk inches deep into their thick necks. Close by two more were dead or dying, dropped by high-speed projectiles from the Karbarrans' air rifles.

"Get him up!" Jack yelled, scrambling to his feet and motioning to Tesla. "Gnea, Bela, check that corridor!"

The Praxian women had crossbows and swords held low as they moved in; Crysta came up behind them with her rifles ready to mete out additional force. Tesla was up now and dusting off his robes.

"Barbarians," he said, looking around at the dead soldiers.

"Save it," Jack spat, giving him a nudge in the gut with the launcher.

Tesla looked down his snout at the Human. For small and primitive beings, he decided, they were possessed of an incredible ferocity at times. And while this in itself was not uncommon, it was completely at variance with the sympathetic, *caring* traits they were so fond of displaying.

Tesla, Jack, Janice, and Learna were nearing the communicator sphere when something suddenly charged the air—a resonant, bone-rattling hum that carried a peculiar odor with it.

"An alert," Tesla announced, fingers on the sphere's activation controls. "Seems you've succeeded in calling attention to yourselves."

"Anything?" Jack called out to Gnea. She shook her head, then offered him a perplexed shrug.

"Ahh, there's the reason they're leaving us alone . . ."

Jack turned around in time to see an image come to life in the heart of the sphere. It took a moment to make sense of the scene, and Learna was the first to gasp.

"Looks as though we've a rebellion on our hands," Tesla ventured.

The sphere showed a virtual army of Garudans pouring into the basin. Invid soldiers were butchering them from dug-in positions close to the base of the hive. The Optera tree forest was ablaze, giving the crater the look of a devil's cauldron.

"It's suicide!"

Janice put her arm around Learna's soft shoulders.

"Then let's make it count for something," Jack said in a determined voice. He nudged Tesla into motion again, and the Invid began to lead them along one of the corridors. Shortly they were standing before a shimmering portal similar to the one at the hive entrance. Once again, Tesla's hand or voice "unlocked" the portal, and the team found themselves in a kind of control center, filled with "furniture"—strangely contoured chairs and fairly conventional tables and countertops—wardrobe closets, instrumentality columns, communicator spheres of various size and design, and what looked to be Tiresian Robotech devices.

The team fanned out to search the space and Lron made an important discovery behind one of the long counters: two cowering white-robed Invid scientists.

The Karbarran pulled them up by their necks and shoved them toward the center of the room.

"Tesla!" one of them seethed, following up with what Jack imagined to be a few choice Invid epithets. Janice translated: "He called Tesla a traitor. Said it was true what they'd heard about him."

"Meaning what?" Jack asked.

"Why, my leading you here," Tesla said too quickly.

"Where is Kami?" Learna demanded.

Tesla put the question to them, then grunted when the scientists had replied. "They refuse to say."

Jack grabbed Crysta's rifle and held it to the head of one of the scientists. "Ask him again."

Tesla listened to the reply and shook his head.

"All right then—"

"Hold it a moment, Jack," Bela interrupted. "Perhaps they crave a lungful of Garuda's fresh air . . ."

Tesla told the two what the Sentinels had in store for them; even Jack could see their snout sensors blanch at the prospect. No one really needed the translation.

"They've changed their minds," Tesla announced with a snort of disapproval.

And with that the scientists began to lead the Sentinels on a circuitous tour through the dome, descending always, via tractor tubes and spiral drops where there should have been stairs, past conveyor systems and vat after vat of Fruits or pulverized stem and Flower, in and out of corridors and rooms, commo stations and rotundas, all recently vacated by soldiers and worker drones who had ceased their tasks to protect the farm. Within minutes of leaving the control center Jack felt completely lost; he had no idea where they were in relation to the hive entrance, and began to wonder whether the scientists were leading them into a trap. But his concern faded by the time they reached what he guessed to be the lowest, perhaps underground level; they had passed numerous places where ambushes could have been sprung, but not a single soldier had been seen. Then at last they reached the end of the line—or so it seemed until one of the scientists actually walked the group *right through a wall*. The chamber beyond was a kind of membranous sac, veined and pulsating like something one might find in an unhealthy lung, and there, heaped together in the center of the floor, were Rick, Lisa, Karen, and Kami.

Fearing the worst, Jack hung back while everyone else ran to them—everyone but Janice, who positioned herself near the sac's osmotic gate where she could keep an eye on Tesla. Learna immediately slipped a transpirator over Kami's muzzle and hugged him to herself for all it was worth. Kami stirred some after a moment, but the three Humans were another matter; sickly pale and disheveled, they languished in a deathlike stupor, whimpering every so often.

"... subjected them to the atmosphere, then performed some sort of mind-probe experiments," Janice could hear Tesla translating.

Janice saw the two scientists take a step back as Jack and the others swung around to them. She pretended to preoccupy herself studying the chamber's portal, furnishing

Tesla with a bit of illusory breathing space. At the same time, she sharpened her eyes and ears in his direction.

"Don't worry about a thing," Tesla was telling his comrades in a low but reassuring tone. "Now that the Regent has been . . . killed, Tesla will rule in his place. I will make peace with these beings and—"

"Tesla, what are you saying?" one of the Invid cut him off. "The Regent killed? We just spoke with him. In fact, it was he who told us to expect you."

"What?" You spoke . . . But, but what you said, what you said about it being true—"

"Yes," the other scientist sneered. "That you had taken up the Sentinels' fight, and that we should beware your treachery!"

"No!" Tesla said too loudly. He caught himself and risked a glance at Janice, but she kept her eyes averted from him.

Jack, Gnea, and Lron were storming up to him when he swung back around. Lron took hold of each of the scientists by the fronts of their robes.

"Ask them what they did with Rem." Jack barked.

Tesla peered over at the rescued group, noticing for the first time the Tiresian was not among them. Absently, he put the question to the two he had hoped were to be his first subjects, still stunned by what they had told him. *The Regent alive? How could it be?*

"Well?" Jack shouted. "What's he saying?"

Tesla waited for the scientist to repeat it, nodding as he listened. "Rem is Tiresian. His dreams were less, shall we say, *commonplace*. So he was sent elsewhere for further tests."

"Where?" Janice asked, walking over to him.

Tesla listened for a moment. "To Haydon IV. In fact, the Regent himself is on his way—" Tesla eyes went wide and the words caught in his throat.

"Go on . . ."

He swallowed and found his voice—raspy as it was, all at once. "The Regent is on his way to Haydon IV as we speak."

"Then that's where we're bound," Bela said evenly, her eyes narrowed to slits.

Tesla gulped, loud enough for everyone to hear.

"We've got to get them to Jean's med team," Learna announced, still holding on to her mate.

Bela lifted Lisa from the floor. "We have no time to lose."

Lron and Crysta moved in to take hold of Rick and Karen.

Max and Miriya received Cabell's good news/bad news update over the com net: Rick and the others had been rescued, but they were still under the effects of the planet's microbe-laden atmosphere and delirious with fever. Moreover, the mission had gone smoothly with no casualties among the team, but Rem was no longer on Garuda. Jack's team was out of the crater hive now and awaiting extraction; Jean claimed that Rick, Lisa, and Karen were too weak to endure the trip back to the med group's temporary hq by Hovercycle or Garudan flitter.

Max signed off and immediately raised two of his wingmen on the tac, ordering them to rendezvous with Skull One at the crater hive. Reconfiguring the mecha to Guardian mode, he imaged the Alpha into a vertical takeoff and set his course northeast for the basin. As the VT rose, Max had a full view of the forests and steppes the Skull and Wolff Pack had turned to wasteland. Not since the battle on Karbarra had he seen so much death, such extensive destruction. The dome-shaped hive was in ruins, collapsed and in flames; the Optera tree forests, along with patches of grassland and evergreen, were burning out of control. The terrain was ravaged beyond belief—pockmarked, holed, cratered, littered with legless or pincerless Invid mecha, bits of Hovertank and Veritech, Bioroid and Inorganic. An entire hillside was covered base to summit with Hellcat husks and Invid and Garudan corpses. Hundreds, perhaps thousands had died. And from what Max was hearing over the net, the same scene had played at each and every Invid farm and installation throughout the planet's equatorial belt. But Garuda had freed itself from the offworlders' yoke.

Good news ... bad news.

Max said as much to Miriya as the VT covered the fifty or so miles to the crater. She was still in the Beta module and apparently all right, in spite of her ordeal. Max was cautiously optimistic; he had yet to quiz her about how her fighter had been brought down in the first place.

The crater hive was for the most part intact, but Max didn't expect it to last much longer. Fires encroaching on it from all sides. Skull One dropped out of the smoke and clouds onto a battleground much like the one they had just left, dead and wounded strewn across the field, a palpable commingling of triumph and loss. Those Invid who had survived were seeing the Garudan's barbaric side; but Max didn't suppose he could fault Kami's people for the day's bloody aftermath, this requisite catharsis.

Masked again, Jack, Gnea, and Bela directed Max and his wingmen in, and got Rick and the others into the VTs as fast as they could. Lron, Crysta, and Janice were keeping Tesla and a few Invid scientists under guard inside the hive—protected from the Garudans' bloodlust for the time being. Kami, still weak but ambulatory now, was off somewhere sharing the bittersweet taste of victory with Learna and their fellow warriors. Mopping up, Max ventured, much as the Wolff Pack was doing in other quarters.

Max caught a brief glimpse of Rick as he was being lifted into the cargo space of Blue Danube's Beta module. The transpirator prevented Max from being able to see his friend's face, but Rick looked as though the Invid had robbed him of his bones.

The three VTs raced for Kami's village, where Jean's team took over and carried Rick and the others to the safety of the geodesic med dome. Max couldn't help but see it as a miniature version of the Invid hives they had just destroyed.

He and Miriya entered on Jack's heels, doffed their masks, and took in a lungful of the dome's artificial atmosphere.

"Sweet, isn't it?" Max said, trying to sound cheerful.

Miriya gave him a weak smile, but said nothing.

He was reaching for her hand when she suddenly stumbled and collapsed into his arms.

Use your discretion, but try to have your men hold off until you're certain that at least half of them [ed. note: the Zentraedi] are inside—that includes Breetai and that kingsize bitch, Kazianna. Instruct the demo team to use more charges than they think necessary; I don't want any of them coming out alive. In fact, it might be worthwhile to sabotage as many of their environment suits as possible beforehand. Neither of us believe in accidents, Adams, but we're going to call it that no matter what.

A "Code Pyramid" communiqué from T. R. Edwards, as quoted in Wildman's *When Evil Had Its Day*

A TIGHT CLUSTER OF LIGHTS WAS DESCENDING OUT of Fantoma's perpetually brooding skies. Breetai watched them for a moment, then turned away from the command center's blister viewport to face his lieutenant.

"They've arrived, my lord."

"So I see," Breetai said soberly. He glanced back over his shoulder, snapped the faceshield that sealed his pressurized armor closed, and moved to the hut's airlock. The lieutenant and two armed soldiers followed him out into Fantoma's night.

A constant debris-filled wind had been scouring the ringed giant's surface for the past three days, and Breetai instinctively raised an arm against it as he marched in lumbering high strides toward the landing zone's illumination grid. Nearly all of the Zentraedi cadre had turned out for the confrontation, and Breetai spied Kazianna Hesh among them. Nearby were a dozen or so Micronians in environment suits—some of Lang's Robotechs. Edwards's Ghost Riders were reconfiguring their Veritechs now, imaging over from Guardian to Battloid as they touched down.

"He apparently has more on his mind than a friendly chat," Breetai said to his lieutenant while the last of the squadron was snapping into upright mode. As murmurs of discontent reached him over the tactical freq, Breetai instructed his first officer to pass the word along that he wouldn't tolerate any incidents; no matter what Edwards said or did, his troops were to keep silent.

Edwards stepped his Battloid off the grid and began to move across the field in Breetai's direction. The Zentraedi knew better than to regard this as some gesture of compromise. Four of the Ghosts flanked Edwards, with a kind of threatening casualness to the way they cradled their rifle/cannons. Breetai threw his lieutenant a knowing glance. The show of force came as no surprise; Dr. Lang had already given him an idea of what to expect.

"New Zarkopolis welcomes General Edwards," Breetai said with practiced elaborateness. "We're sorry we couldn't provide the general with better weather." He could hear a few Zentraedi snicker.

"Very thoughtful of you," Edwards returned over the mecha's external speakers, mimicking Breetai's tone of voice. "And I'm sorry I can't bring you better news."

The two men fell into an uneasy silence; the wind came up, howling and pinging gravel against Breetai's armored suit and the Battloid's alloy. The Zentraedi commander narrowed his eyes and grinned, picturing Edwards in the mecha's cockpit, nervous hands on the controls. When one of the VT's gauntlets came up, Breetai almost made a grab for it, but restrained himself at the last moment. Edwards caught the gesture, however.

"A bit nervous today, are we, Breetai?"

Breetai snorted. "This wind has put me in a foul humor."

Edwards inclined the ultratech knight's head. "Well then, maybe this won't seem like bad news after all." The mecha's hand held out an outsize audio device for Breetai's inspection. "You and your...*crew* are relieved, Commander. New Zarkopolis is now under REF jurisdiction, and I'll be assuming personal control of this facility. Tomorrow's cargo run will be your last. You can hear it straight from the council, if you wish."

The Zentraedi began to grumble among themselves, and Edwards's sentries took a step forward. Breetai motioned his cadre silent with a downward wave of his massive hand. He accepted the playback device and regarded it for a moment. "No need for that. But I should warn you, General, that you're going to find the conditions here somewhat harsh. This is, after all, *Zentraedi's* work."

Edwards's short laugh issued from the speakers. "We'll manage all right. Of course, you're all welcome to stay on—as *laborers*, you understand."

"I'll consider it, General."

"Good, Breetai, good," Edwards said, pleased with the outcome. "I like a man who can follow orders. Could be that you and I will see eye to eye yet."

Breetai nodded, tight-lipped. Peripherally, he noticed Kazianna stepping deliberately into his restricted field of view.

Edwards went on to inform him that within a week's time several hundred men and women would begin arriving from Tirol, along with the new mecha Lang's teams had designed. Until then, Edwards was leaving behind six of his troops to oversee the transfer of command. *Six or six hundred,* Breetai said to himself, *it wouldn't matter now.*

When Edwards and most of his squadron had lifted off, Breetai swung stiffly into the wind and made for the mining colony's Quonset-style headquarters. On the way, he asked the lieutenant if his men had completed their task.

"Almost, my lord."

"And the fool's ore?"

"Loaded for tomorrow's delivery."

Breetai grunted. "See to it that the last of the monopole is placed aboard the ship. The delivery will go as scheduled, but the monopole remains our property."

The lieutenant raised an eyebrow. "About Edwards's soldiers, Commander..."

Breetai came to a halt short of the headquarters hatchway. "Invite them along to 'oversee' the delivery. Afterward, we'll give them the option of joining us."

"And if they refuse?"

"I leave that up to you," Breetai said, stepping inside.

"Pregnant?" Max asked, as Rhestad's morning rays touched the med team's geodesic shelter.

Vince shrugged his huge shoulders. "That's what Jean says. And Cabell concurs."

"That's right, my boy," Cabell affirmed. "It is most remarkable, but true." The Tiresian was all smiles for a change, his concern for Rem momentarily eclipsed. "I thought her first pregnancy the exception that proved the rule. But this—this is nothing short of..."

"Remarkable," Max finished for him, shaking his head in disbelief. "Yeah, tell me about it."

Vince laughed. "What's with you? It takes two, if I'm not mistaken."

Max looked up into Vince's brown face. "Yeah, but.. Vince, you don't understand. Remember, Miriya's.. *different.*"

"She had Dana," Vince started to say.

"Yeah, and Dana's *different.*"

"How is she different?" Cabell wanted to know.

Max and Vince traded looks, but left the question unanswered. "Can I see her?" Max said suddenly, getting up.

Vince laughed. "That's a good start."

Max started off for the small area of the med dome Jean's team had partitioned off.

"Remarkable," Cabell mused as he and Vince walked back to where Rick, Lisa, and Karen were undergoing treatment. The three had yet to emerge from semiconsciousness...

"Any change?" Vince asked his wife a moment later. She was standing over Rick just now, looking almost as drawn and pale as her patient. Vince put his arm around her narrow waist.

"I'm worried, Vince. They should have come out of it by now. We've tried everything—antipsychotics, transfusions . . ." She threw up her hands. "I don't know what to do."

"It is the *hin*," Veidt said, hovering over to them from the foot of Karen's bed. He had spent the last several hours absorbing everything Jean's medical library databanks had to offer. "Garudans live in the womb of the *hin*. It is what you might term 'an alternate reality.' The microorganisms here, the same which keep Kami's people in a constant state of *hin*, have caused your friends to become *unstuck* in what constitutes *Human* reality."

"Yes, and it's killing them, Veidt. It's not providing them with psychedelic trips or allies or personal power. It's draining the life from them while we sit here and . . . and—"

"Come on, Jean," Vince said. "You're doing what you can."

Cabell tugged at his beard. "There is a treatment, of course." He turned to Veidt as Vince and Jean's eyes fixed on him.

"I will be succinct," the Haydonite began. "On my world there are devices capable of reversing the Garudan effect. 'Mental illness,' as some of your disks name it, is unknown to us; it is as archaic a thing as your own smallpox."

"Then what are we waiting for?" Jean said, looking up at Vince. "Our work here is finished, isn't it? Garuda's liberated."

Vince removed his hand from her waist to feel his jaw. "Yes, in a way."

"In a way? What's that supposed to mean?"

"We've learned that the Regent is on his way to Haydon IV," Cabell told her. "With what remains of his fleet, no doubt."

Jean compressed her lips. "More fighting, then."

"It's not even as *simple* as that," Vince added.

"Our world," Veidt said, "cannot be approached with the same tactics you employed to liberate Karbarra, Praxis, and Garuda. Haydon IV is in a certain sense beyond both conquest or liberation. And while it is true that the Invid have assumed control of our political structure, they have not in any way attempted to tamper with our lives. They *could not*. Haydon IV is an open world and will always remain so."

"Couldn't we sneak through or something? I mean, isn't there a back door we could use, some way of getting to those devices without confronting the Invid?"

Veidt stared at Jean and shook his head. "It is impossible."

Vince was pacing up and down, hands clasped behind his back. "We've gotta ask ourselves whether it's worth the risk."

"Whether Rick, Lisa, and Karen are worth the risk, you mean."

"And Rem," Cabell added.

Vince nodded.

"Look what you've already risked to save them," Veidt pointed out.

Everyone fell silent; then Vince said, "Gather the Sentinels. We've got a decision to make."

"I will not have him here! I will not!" the Regis railed to one of her servants. *Was there no escaping him?* she asked herself. *Even here on Haydon IV?*

"I'm afraid it's too late, Your Grace," the servant said, unmoved from its posture of genuflection. "The Regent's flagship has already left Optera to rendezvous here with the remnants of his fleet."

"How long do I have?" she asked, whirling on the sexless creature, the tassels of her long gloves whipping about.

"Less than one period, Your Grace."

She dismissed the servant; when it left the room, she clenched her fists and waved them in the air. "Must he stalk me?" she said aloud. "Must he continue to punish me?"

Abruptly, she turned around to regard Rem; the Zorclone was asleep, perhaps unconscious after his sessions with the Regent's scientists from Garuda. They had cured him of the madness induced by that world's atmosphere, only to induce a more controlled state of hallucinatory dread. And then they had picked his brain. *Oh, how they had picked his brain.*

For the better part of five days now the Regis had had him much to herself; hers to toy with, hers to examine— his dreams and thoughts to dissect, his memories to relive ... United with him on some psychic plane, she had walked again through those fields they had walked on Optera. Old Optera, Optera before the fall. She had been able to view those times through his eyes now, and had found herself stirred. He had seen how much she wanted to emulate him, in every way; and she had seen how much he had desired her. Not her physical being, not the form destiny had wed her to, but her spiritual self—her *essence*. There was at one time a semblance of love there, and this discovery filled her with joy. But it was a rapture that could not survive the realities his war-hungry race had introduced into her garden; a rapture that could only endure on that etheric plane, where things cast beautiful but ultimately painful shadows ...

Still she could hardly tear herself away from that realm, even though her self-indulgence might mean death for the clone. He was her plaything; much as she had been Zor's!

She understood, however, that Zor had somehow meant to redeem himself by sending the Protoculture matrix far from his Masters' reach. But much of this remained unclear, muddled by what she had accessed from Haydon IV's data systems. These grand designs again: Zor, the Masters, the Invid, all locked together in some immense, unfathomable framework.

Along with this mysterious blue-white world revealed by the clone's thoughts, this nexus of events, this pleroma ...

She had yet to learn either the name of the planet or its continuum coordinates, but she now had a sense of where to begin her search. And sooner or later her sensor nebulae would locate it.

I will follow the nebulae, she decided all at once. *I will quit this Quadrant and place myself as far from his reach as that matrix was from the Masters' evil embrace.*

She found herself excited by the prospect, laughing as she overlooked Haydon IV's artificial land-and cityscapes. She could even leave some of her Children behind until the moment arrived—the moment when that blue-white world was discovered and made her own!

She increased her size, towering up to fill the room, knowing a determination she had thought lost with love itself. Regarding Rem, she said, "Now let the Regent have his way with you, clone. Let him peer into your memories of our time together, and let him suffer for what he missed!"

Miriya did not look as well as Max had imagined she might. Where was that rosy glow, that special something? Instead, she seemed wasted; baggy-eyed, bone-weary, even slightly jaundiced.

"It's just from my exposure to the atmosphere," Miriya told him as he carefully sat down on the edge of her cot. "But Jean says everything's fine, all systems go. So smooth your wrinkled brow, my darling, and kiss me before I do something violent."

Max forced a smile and leaned into her arms; they held each other for a moment. Max patted her back and straightened up. "I'm not sure I know what to feel," he confessed.

"I know, Max. I'm just as concerned as you are about Rick and Lisa."

"Good news, bad news . . ."

"That's life, Max. And now Dana's going to have a sister."

Max's brows went up. "Jean tell you that?"

"She didn't have to." Miriya caressed her belly. "I can sense it."

Again, Max tried to feel good about things, but the more he looked at his wife, the more anxious he became. He was about to take her hand, when someone rapped against the partition. Crysta, Gnea, and Teal asked if they could come in for a moment. The Spherisian was carrying the infant—a two-foot Baldan, although still faceted and speechless as yet.

"As soon as I heard the news I came down," Teal explained. "I wanted you to see the infant."

"Congratulations," Gnea said to Miriya uncertainly.

"Hey, what about the father?" Max asked good-naturedly.

The Praxian turned to him. "Why? Did you have something to do with Miriya's condition?"

Max started to respond, but thought better of it, shutting his mouth and blinking stupidly.

"When does he become smooth, like you?" Miriya was saying to Teal.

"It doesn't. It's not necessarily a he."

Miriya looked around uncomfortably. "But I thought that Baldan . . . that this . . ."

"It is of Baldan," Teal replied, regarding the infant analytically. "But the features and what I think you call 'the sex' are ultimately left to the Shaper."

"The Shaper? You?" Crysta said, surprised, one huge paw to her muzzle.

"Who else? The young Spherisian remains faceted until smoothed by its Shaper. Soon I will de-facet it."

"But you'll shape him, er, it in Baldan's image, won't you?"

"Why would I do that? I am bonded with the infant now. I could just as easily shape it in my own image."

"But this is all that remains of Baldan," Crysta argued. "Don't you want to recapture his essence? It would mean much to all of us."

Miriya and Gnea agreed. Max kept out of it.

"Among Spherisians I am considered most attractive,"

Teal told them proudly. "A young one could do far worse than be shaped as I am." She regarded Max and Miriya a moment. "You Earthers don't even have a choice in the matter."

"No argument there." Max laughed. "But maybe that's the beauty of it."

Gnea made a face, astonishment in her gold-flecked eyes. "So you *did* have something to do with it."

Max looked from Praxian, to Karbarran, to Spherisian, to his own Zentraedi wife, and wondered if he could possibly explain himself.

The Zentraedi's cargo transport—named the *Valivarre* for Fantoma's primary—was the largest of the ships constructed to serve the needs of the mining op. It was essentially an enormous shell, with vast featureless cabinspaces and cargo holds, and numerous launch and docking bays sized to accommodate ranks of surface mecha and outsize shuttles. Typical of the new breed SDFs—4 through 8—the *Valivarre* was only lightly armed and somewhat slow by galactic standards; but unlike those fortresses the ship was equipped with Protoculture/Reflex drives that enabled it to astrogate near-instantaneous folds throughout "local space."

The transport was in stationary orbit over Tirol just now, off-loading the latest of Fantoma's riches to cargo shuttles, which were making runs both to the SDF-3 and to the moon's surface.

On the *Valivarre*'s bridge, Breetai was informed that one of the returning shuttles was bringing up two passengers. He arrived in the busy docking bay just as Dr. Lang and Exedore were descending the shuttle ramp.

Lang took a look around. Under the watchful gaze of four Ghost Squadron Battloids, a dozen Zentraedi were loading the last of the monopole ore into a second shuttle. There was more noise than Human ears were meant to withstand, so he donned a pair of silencer muffs, and went on the amplibox to communicate with Breetai.

"It appears that everything is in order, Commander," he said, trying to sound businesslike. "But I have some matters to discuss with you regarding the transfer schedule. Is there somewhere we can talk?"

Breetai led them out of the hold and into a small cabin-space outfitted with a Micronian commo balcony.

"This area is secure," Breetai told them after he had dogged the hatch.

Lang got right to the point. "You'll never get away with this, Breetai. What do you take us for?"

The Zentraedi grinned. "The fool's ore . . . It wasn't my intention to trick you, Lang. Only Edwards's men. As far as they are concerned, we are off-loading the monopole."

"But, Commander," Exedore said, "what are you trying to accomplish? You're aware that Lang and I will have to report this."

"And I fully expect you to. I ask only that you delay your report for three hours."

"You're leaving!" Lang said, excited. "I knew it."

Breetai folded his arms across his chest and nodded. "That's right, Doctor. We're leaving. And we're taking the monopole with us."

Lang was shaking his head. "It's a mad scheme, Breetai. Edwards will hunt you down."

"Perhaps. But he'll think twice about firing on us while we have the ore aboard. Not when he learns that Fantoma's yield is exhausted. I'm relying on you to make this clear to him."

"Commander, may we enquire—"

"To search for Admiral Hunter, Exedore. I don't accept that the Sentinels have become outlaws any more than I believe the Invid Regent is dead. We know that enemy, Exedore; we engaged them throughout this sector. If he had been assassinated, his queen's troops would have already massed against Tirol and atomized it." Breetai leaned closer to the balcony railing to regard his Micronized friend. "We are free of all imperatives now, Exedore. The Zentraedi will follow none but their own. Will you join us?"

Exedore bowed his head. "Commander, you honor me. But I, too, have an inner imperative."

Breetai mulled it over, then nodded. "I understand, my friend."

Lang looked at the two Zentraedi, suddenly aware of the import the moment held. A surge of misgiving washed through him; a shaping charge he could barely sustain. His voice cracked when he spoke. "To Praxis, Breetai? Garuda? Spheris? The ship you seek is small enough as to be insignificant."

Breetai fixed his eye on Lang. "I don't believe that, Doctor. Nor do you."

Lang rasped, "Haydon IV." *She is there*, something told him.

Exedore stretched out a hand. "Doctor—"

"Don't ask me to explain." Was it Janice, he wondered, or some other *she*? It was a presence the Shaping had alerted him to, a power unlike anything he had experienced . . .

Breetai regarded him for a moment. "I will begin my search there."

Lang nodded, weakly, wondering whether he would ever see the Zentraedi again.

On Garuda, the Sentinels grouped together in the longhouse to discuss their options and priorities, which meant that it was back to transpirators for almost everyone involved. Vince, Max, and Jack were so certain of where they stood that they had already had Rick, Lisa, and Karen brought up to the SDF-7. Under Wolff's and Janice's supervision, Tesla and the two Invid scientists had also been moved to the ship, along with Miriya—who was still too weak to take part in the meeting—and Teal and the Spherisian infant.

Most of Garuda was celebrating—the grieving would come later—and the wild sounds of song and dance made it all the more difficult for the group to come to any agreement concerning the Haydon IV option. They did find themselves united, however, on the issue of Garuda. With the Optera tree orchards in ruins, it wasn't likely that the Invid were going to have much use for the planet—especially not when their initial campaign against Garuda's inherent defenses had ended in so many deaths. But just in case the Regent decided to think along the lines of reprisals—which, Cabell maintained, was highly unlikely given the disastrous defeats the Invid leader had been suffering in other quarters—the Sentinels were prepared to leave most of their forces onworld to complement the strength of the remaining Bioroid clones. The one Invid hive that had come through the battle reasonably intact would serve as their base. Vince and Veidt were in favor of this even though it would significantly reduce the Sentinels' firepower. Haydon IV, though, was not be thought of in terms of a military campaign; they were undertaking the journey for the sake of Rick, Lisa, Karen, and Rem.

Once again, as someone pointed out.

But the Karbarrans and Praxians, in any case, chose to disregard Vince's statement. They likewise ignored Veidt and Sarna's claim that the planet had not been adversely affected by the Invid presence. Haydon IV had Invid; therefore, Haydon IV needed to be liberated.

Kami and Learna were reluctant to leave, reluctant to abandon the *hin* and to have to reattach themselves to life-support systems; but they agreed to see things through to their completion after Lron and Crysta reminded them of how they had left their son, Dardo, behind on Karbarra.

The Sentinels were back to the core group.

And they were also back to unknowns.

It was possible they might beat the Regent's fleet to Haydon IV; get in and out without incident. But it was just as likely that things would continue in the same unpredictable fashion they had grown accustomed to.

Ten Earth-standard hours later, the SDF-7 left orbit and jumped.

FOURTEEN

While it was true the Invid had been existing on the very same fruits and flowers that were rapidly turning Tesla into something not-quite or more-than Invid, it must be pointed out that the liquified plant-stuff which reached Optera was of a "pasteurized" variety, and was principally utilized as nutrient bath for the soldiers' battle mecha—Scouts, Shock Troopers, Pincer Ships, and such. By forcing himself to subsist on the pure (or the impure, in actuality), Tesla was receiving megadoses of the same stuff that years earlier had sent the Zentraedi Khyron clear over the edge of the Imperative, and into undreamed-of states of metanoia.

History of the Second Robotech War, volume XXXVI "Tirol"

"I DEMAND TO KNOW WHERE SHE IS!" THE REGENT bawled as he and his eleven-trooper elite stormed across one of Haydon IV's ice-blue plazas, the splendors of the city lost on them.

The planet's indigenous beings paid the Invid little mind, and went about their mysterious business, hovering in groups of two or three in and out of Glike's spirelike buildings, across graceful bridges, and through parks too perfect to believe. But visitors, guests, and merchants from other worlds stopped to gaze upon the one whose race had most recently changed the face of the Fourth Quadrant. A few Karbarrans even had to be restrained from running forward to mock the Regent with reminders of their recent victory. "Sentinels! Sentinels!" they chanted, and succeeded for a moment in bringing the Regent around to confront them. No one, however, dared make a violent move, for beneath those very same plazas and parks lurked surprises of a decidedly punishing nature. Haydon IV had rules for citizens and strangers alike, and it enforced them without bias.

The Invid squad commander whispered as much to the Regent, while the ursine Karbarrans continued to hurl insults and imprecations. And at the same moment one of the Regis's servants approached, offering a brief and unconvincing genuflection.

"Your Highness," the servant said, with a condescending tone.

The Regent raised a fist. "How dare she refuse to honor my arrival!"

"Perhaps, my lord," the Regent's own lieutenant suggested, "she trembles in terror at the mere thought of your blinding presence."

"Grovel on your own time," the Regent snarled. He fixed his wife's servant with a gimlet stare. "Where is my shameful wife? Explain this breach of protocol, worm, before I find a place for you in the Pits."

The servant lifted its head. "She is gone, Regent."

The Regent knew as much already, and bristled at the servant's impertinence. "I'm aware that she is gone—her flagship has left orbit. But I want to know *where*."

"She left no word, m'lord. Save to say that she is not expected to return."

"Which explains your laxity." The Regent raised himself to his full height, and looked down his snout on the Regis's creature. "Perhaps I will make an example of you, grub. Now, lead me to our chambers before I forget myself ... See that my pets are cared for," he said to his lieutenant as an afterthought, "and have the Sentinel prisoner brought before me."

Several other servants appeared to usher the Regent and his retinue to the same rooms his queen had occupied and abandoned, and along the way he could not help but take note of some of Haydon IV's wonders. The planet was unlike anything he had ever seen, and yet there was a sense of familiarity everywhere he looked. Here, a structure that was reminiscent of Tiresia; there, a patch of forest seemingly lifted from Garuda. Spherisian crystal palaces, Kar-

barran factories without the dirt or stench, Praxian ara-
besque carvings, totems, statues, pillars, and pedestals—
even some things which could only have come from Optera
itself: fields of Flowers and rows of Fruit-bearing trees, all
sterile to be sure, but so faultless, so *exquisite* in appearance.

And yet nowhere a hint of instrumentality.

He understood, though, why the Regis would leave:
there was no warmth to the world, no taste of life to its
clear skies and reflective waters. No, she would not have
been at home here, he told himself. It was a *real* world she
required, one like the Optera of their past. He refused to
believe that his arrival could have forced her hand—certainly not after the *gift* he had sent her. This, however,
didn't stop him from complaining to his lieutenant once
they had reached the tall spire's uppermost rooms and his
throne had been positioned.

"Decamped!" he sneered, hands stroking the gem-
collared necks of his Hellcat pets. "She expects me to win
the war while she's off flitting around the cosmos preening
her tubercles and hatching plots against me—"

"M'lord," a servant interrupted, bowing from the doorway. "We have the prisoner."

The Regent smiled as Rem was dragged in. A lieutenant
"persuaded" the Tiresian to assume a groveling posture.
But the Regent's smile began to fade as he studied Rem.
Great suns! he thought. *He does wear the face of the se-
ducer!*

Two scientists had entered on the heels of the Zor-
Clone, and the 'Cats were suddenly snarling, pacing, and
sniffing the air. "What did she think of him?" the Regent
asked, rising from his chair.

One of the scientists made a coughing sound. "Uh, she
was . . . *amused*, Your Highness."

"Yes, I can well imagine. Did you record their sessions
together?"

The two Invid traded quick glances. "We did, my lord."

He turned to gaze at Rem. "I wish to view the results of

their reunion. I want to see her guilt, the sadness in her heart, before I grant her forgiveness."

"But, Regent—"

The Regent slammed a massive fist down on the throne's contoured seat. "Bring me the recordings—*now!*"

There was silence on the bridge of the SDF-7 while Wolff and Vince waited for the ship's identification library to display its assessment. Wolff folded his arms and leaned away from the console when the data appeared.

"Well?"

"Signatures confirmed," Wolff said flatly. "Invid troop carriers the Regent's flagship. We're too late."

"Are they scanning us?"

Wolff exhaled loudly and swung to a peripheral monitor. "Affirmative. But it's low-level, cursory. Could be we're an unknown quantity. God knows there are enough other ships docked out here."

Vince had to agree; he had never seen so many different types and classes of starship. Haydon IV was obviously all that Veidt and Sarna had been telling everyone.

"So what do we do, Captain—open a hailing frequency, tell them we're just in for liberty, a little R 'n' R?"

Vince frowned and put a hand on the ship's address-system stud . . .

"Haydon IV is an open world," Veidt was explaining in the briefing room ten minutes later. "I thought I had already made myself clear on this point. The planet has never been taken by force; its defenses are legendary. There are, in the central records, references to an attempted invasion some two thousand Earth-standard years ago. Several hundred vessels were destroyed in a matter of moments."

"But the Invid—" Jack started to say.

"The Invid did not engage Haydon IV's defenses," Sarna picked up. "Any who come in peace are free to stay and trade. The Invid came and insinuated themselves into positions of political authority; but they are quite tame

here. We may land in safety, but we will surely be taken
into custody."

"Then we can't go in under arms," Crysta said.

Jack grunted. "Maybe you don't have the courage to try,
but I do."

Lron glared at him from across the table. "You dare
impugn her courage? Perhaps you—"

"Stop this!" Jean interrupted. "Both of you."

"Exactly what are these 'defenses,' Veidt?" Vince
wanted to know.

"I have never seen them. As I stated, they have not been
put to the test in two thousand of your years."

"Come on," Jack said, looking around. "Then how do
we know they're still functioning?"

"Do you hunger to challenge them?" Sarna asked.

Jack returned a sullen stare.

Jean shook her head and snorted. "So to utilize the medical facilities, we have to go in with our hands raised."

"Yes, straight into an Invid stronghold," Bela said.

"We are given no choice," Gnea added. "Our comrades
will have to be surrendered. But who among us will escort
them down?" The Praxian glanced around the table.

"I'll go," Wolff volunteered.

Jean caught her husband's eye. "I will, too."

"Wait a minute, wait a minute," Jack said, standing up.
"I'm as concerned about Karen and Rick and Lisa as any of
you. But just suppose the Invid deny the request for medical help. Then they've not only got Karen, they've got you
and you and whoever else is crazy enough to volunteer."
He shook his head. "Uh, uh. We need to find some way
around this."

"The Invid cannot deny that which is promised by the
planet to all," Veidt said, loud enough to cut through all the
separate arguments Jack's objection had raised. Everyone
heard the Haydonite's remark, but the bickering continued.

"All right, simmer down," Vince told the table. "Max
has an idea."

"Two landing parties," the Skull ace began when everyone was quiet. He was exhausted, having spent every min-

ute by Miriya's side. Her condition had deteriorated after the fold to Haydon IV, and it was Jean's thought to number her among the patients. "Some of us take the four of them down; the rest of you go in unannounced to keep an eye on us."

"It will not work, Commander," Veidt said; but Jack, Lron, Bella, and Gnea were already enthusiastic. Even Burak added his voice to the group as a show of support.

"The planet's defenses will detect you," Sarna tried to warn them. "We'll have to risk it," Vince answered her.

And the plan was put to a vote.

Jean and Wolff had already volunteered, and now Max and Vince and Cabell joined them. Veidt and Sarna would escort them. Jack, however, insisted that Karen's cause would be better served by his *doing* something more than crying by her bedside; so he opted for the second team. Burak, Kami and Learna, Bela, Gnea, Lron, and Crysta threw in with him. Janice was undecided until the last minute; then she allied herself with Jack's group—on one condition: that they take Tesla and the two Invid scientists along with them.

"He did help out back on Garuda," Jack was willing to concede. "But I still don't trust him."

"I don't either," Janice said. "I'd just like to see what would happen if Tesla and the Regent came snout-to-snout."

Only Wolff heard Burak's gasp; but he didn't think anything of it.

"Breetai and his Zentraedi are traitors and criminals," T. R. Edwards told the council, positioning himself where he was certain the cameras would close in on his polished skullplate and furious expression. "They've stolen the very thing we need to return to Earth, and thereby condemned our world to defeat at the hands of the Robotech Masters." He swung around and walked angrily back to his seat, facing the audience now. "Some of you are probably thinking that this is the Zentraedi's way of avenging themselves on the RDF. But I suspect they have an even darker purpose in mind. It's my belief that Breetai means to band together with the Sentinels and form a cartel to take control of the spaceways.

"And with the Invid Regent dead and our own forces stranded, there will be little to stop them from putting their plans in motion—unless we take quick and decisive action against them. For this reason, I'm asking for the council approval of my request for the four ships that comprise our new flotilla. The Zentraedi must be hunted down and destroyed!"

There were conflicting reactions from the crowd, all of which Senator Longchamps silenced with three determined gavel blows. "The council will not tolerate these continued outbursts," he warned the audience. "If this occurs again, I'm going to order the room cleared. Now," he said, turning to Edwards, "the council appreciates the generals's concern, but there are a few issues that need to be addressed." He consulted his notes, then said, "Mr. Obstat?"

"Isn't it true, General, that action of the sort you propose could quite possibly jeopardize the very ore we're so desperately in need of?"

Edwards stood up. "Do you propose to let them have it, then?" he asked evenly.

"We don't know why they took it in the first place," Justine Huxley argued. "I for one am not convinced that they mean to do as you suggest—band together with the Sentinels and embark on some sort of transgalactic campaign. Can't we simply continue to mine ore until the Zentraedi make their demands known to us?"

Dr. Lang spoke to that. "I'm afraid that Fantoma has yielded up the last of its monopole ores. Only trace quantities remain, and further mining is hardly justified at this stage."

"What about our reserves, Doctor, here and on Tirol," Harry Penn asked. "Don't we have enough to repair the fortress's fold systems?"

"Unfortunately not," Exedore asserted. "The . . . *stolen* ore represented more than three months of mining. It is crucial to our goals."

Edwards waited for the gasps and buzzing in the room to subside. "With the council's indulgence, I have reason to question Dr. Lang and Ambassador Exedore's assessment of the situation. It's no secret to the RDF that both of them have special interests in furthering the Sentinels' cause—"

Longchamps banged his gavel. "General, I must caution you to refrain from using this session to cast aspersions on any members of this council. Is that understood?"

The cameras tracked in to catch Edwards's stiff and silent nod.

In Edwards's chambers aboard the SDF-3, where she was watching the proceedings, Minmei got up to fix herself another drink. Lang's face was on-screen when she returned to the edge of the bed.

"That's true, Senator," the Robo-wiz was saying. "Exedore and I were the first to discover that the material offloaded from the *Valivarre* was a type of 'fool's ore,' if you will. We immediately reported this to General Edwards—"

"*After* that ship had folded out of Tirolspace, Doctor," Edwards barked.

"General Edwards," Longchamps cut in, "weren't some of your own Ghost Squadron aboard the *valivarre* supervising the transfer?"

Minmei saw Edwards's face drain of color; the cameras captured the fury in his single eye. "I'm certain that those brave men were killed, Senator."

The cameras cut to Lang. "Council members, I can personally attest to the presence of the general's men. And Exedore and I both found them very much alive."

Minmei sipped her drink, anticipating Edwards's comeback; he didn't surprise her.

"Yes, and exactly *what* motivated you and the ambassador to shuttle up to the *Valivarre*, Doctor?"

"We were merely going over the transfer schedule with Commander Breetai—"

Minmei touched the remote and the screen went blank. She drained her glass and thought, *A few more of these and I'll be too numb to care.* And numb was just what she was after. She had lost her friends, her faith, her voice, any sense of purpose she might have once called her own. Rick, Lisa, Janice, Dr. Lang, Jonathan . . . And lately she had even been thinking about Kyle. She wasn't sure why, but guessed that it had something to do with Edwards and the control he had begun to assert over her. She imagined she saw a curious pattern at work that coupled Rick and Lynn-Kyle, now Jonathan Wolff and Edwards—some slide into self-abuse when she came too close to genuine love and commitment. *Property,* she thought in disgust. That was how she was beginning to view herself. Her voice co-opted by the RDF, her dreams destroyed by war, her will at the mercy of men who wanted nothing more than to rule and posses her, body and mind.

Numb, *comfortably* numb, she told herself . . .

Thirty minutes later the door hissed open and Edwards strode into the room, grinning evilly. Minmei realized she had dozed off, and, startled now, she began to back herself onto the bed. Edwards leered at her, perhaps thinking she was toying with him, and came down on top of her, elbows supporting his upper body. She pressed her hands against his chest and said, "Please . . ."

"What's the matter with you?" he asked, face-to-face with her.

"I'm just . . . confused." She tried to roll out from under him, but his arms held her fast.

"Oh, no, you don't," he told her, bringing his mouth hard against hers—a kiss he liked to think passionate, but one she felt was simply rough. "The council gave their okay."

"W-what does that mean—that you're going to—"

"Precisely that," he said, rolling off her onto his back.

He gazed at the ceiling and laughed. "First the Zentraedi, then the Sentinels." He looked over at her.

Minmei was aghast, gaping at him; he had his right hand curled tightly around her left wrist.

"When this is over I want you to marry me."

Her right hand flew to her face. "What!"

"It'll be just like the Hunters' wedding," he said, as

though thinking aloud. "Except it'll be you and me, and the destination won't be Tirol, but Earth." His grin was still intact.

"And the mission won't be for peace, but for *war!*" she screamed at all once, yanking her arm away.

Edwards sat straight up as she made a move for the door. "What are you talking about? Minmei!"

She was slightly drunk and clumsy even through her fear and shock; she bumped against a table, sending some tapes to the floor, crashed against the bulkhead, fumbling for the door release.

"Minmei!" he yelled again, more harshly than before.

He was angry now and she was panicked. She left the room and ran barefooted along the ship's corridor. She heard someone behind her as she entered the elevator and swung around; but it wasn't Edwards. It was a VT pilot, wearing his helmet, oddly enough, a tall and slender bearded man she thought she had seen before. He was regarding her bare feet and disheveled appearance. She forced a trembling, smile, pushing and patting her hair back in place.

"Troubles?" he said.

"Yes," she told him, surprising herself.

"Anything I can do?"

"I need to get back to Tiresia. Are any shuttles leaving soon?"

"I'll take you myself," he said after a moment.

It made her laugh. "What—in an Alpha? I don't know . . .

"I'll take you wherever you want to go."

She stared at him, wondering why she was ready to believe him. "How about Garuda or Haydon IV . . . uh, 666-60-937?" she asked, reading the pilot's REF service number from his helmet.

"Long trip," he told her. But he didn't laugh, didn't think she was putting him on.

The elevator doors opened. The pilot extended his hand and Minmei allowed herself to take hold of it.

* * *

"A simulagent, a simulagent," Tesla mumbled, stuffing the last of Garuda's Fruits into his mouth. "I've been tricked—*tricked*!"

The two scientists the Sentinels had captured from Garuda backed themselves toward what they hoped would be a safe corner of the dimensional fortress's hold, certain that Tesla's ingestion of the mutated Fruits from that *infected* world had driven him half mad. First there was all that nonsense about the Regent being dead, and now this talk of simulagents and assassination.

"Has he been doing this everywhere you've been?" one of the Invid asked Burak in the lingua franca.

"Only on Karbarra, Praxis, and Garuda so far," the Perytonian devil said in low tones, shrugging. "I suppose his killing the Regent was nothing but an imagining, then—"

"*An imagining!*" Tesla had heard Burak's whisper and swung around to the three of them, monstrous in his anger. He knows that I tried, he knows that I'm out to usurp his throne . . . And I shall have it, do you hear me?! Tesla will *rule*!"

"He's going to get us all sent to the Pits," one of the scientists groaned. "We won't be repatriated—we'll be *devolved*!"

Something, some force, suddenly brought Tesla to his feet. Tesla's skin was rippling, muscles and sinews contorting beneath the flesh as though his internal systems were rearranging themselves, reconfiguring. An aura of light was swirling around his head, throwing rainbow colors across the ceiling, bulkheads, and floor of the hold. His head was listed, neck stretched out, mouth agape in a kind of silent scream. Burak stood rooted to the floor, astonished as he watched the Invid begin to lose stature and bulk, while at the same time Tesla's neck, head, arms, hands, and feet reshaped themselves. The two scientists had buried their heads against one another, but Burak was too awed to summon the will even to look away. He saw then what the Fruits were after, the final form they tried to birth, and he could hardly believe his eyes, much less grasp what such a transformation meant. For the shape was a *humanoid* one—like that of Jack Baker or Gnea or Rem.

Tendrils of energy were whirling around Tesla, reaching out to Burak where he stood. They danced between his horns and sent a downward rush of paralyzing light through the top of his head. Tesla's eyes were fixed on his as something beyond language coursed between them. Burak stiffened, as a cold fire engulfed his heart. He bellowed, and Janice came rushing through the hatch.

She had been outside listening to their muffled exchange, and though baffled by the sudden silence, she had not wanted to risk tipping her hand. Burak's animallike wail had changed all that, but now she couldn't see what was happening. Something or someone was throwing blinding, colored light across the hold. She could make out Burak and the two shadowy shapes of the Invid scientists behind him, but Tesla was concealed by the dazzling prismatic intensity, seemingly at the center of it. She brought her hands to her face, trying to shield her eyes, and all at once the light was gone. Tesla was on the floor, flat on his back.

She rushed over to him; he was alive, but his breathing was labored. And something else: he looked different. His snout was shorter, his head more defined, his hands and feet more humanoid than reptilian. His skin was a pale green, waxy and smooth.

"What happened to him?" Janice asked, turning around to Burak.

The Perytonian stared at her. "I . . . I . . ."

Janice took him by the arms and shook him. "What happened?"

Burak cleared his head and gave her a blank look. He reached up to feel his horns, then regarded Tesla for a moment. "I think he ate too much."

The Regent sat slumped in his throne, feeling as though some great weight had been placed on his chest. It was a mistake for him to have viewed the recordings of the Regis's nostalgic lovefest with the Zor-clone, a terrible mistake. Looking for guilt, for some sign of regret, he had found only love, genuine and unfulfilled. And he began to wonder if he hadn't been wrong in not following her lead when there was still time; when she had pleaded with him to allow himself to be evolved. But he had been stubborn about it, hurt, unforgiving, and now she was lost to him. He had seen, too, the Zor-clone's memories of a world far removed from Optera and Tirol's strife, linked somehow to the Protoculture matrix planet was anything more than Zor's fanciful imaginings? Besides, he had good reason to believe that the Regis had gone off in search of that very world, and he would know if and when she found it. No, what he needed was accurate data, data the clone had not yet surrendered up to Haydon IV's mind-probe devices. Perhaps, he thought, it would have to be *conjured* from the clone, the way Zor had conjured protoculture from the Flowers of Life.

In the meantime, however, his empire was crumbling. Garuda had fallen to the Sentinels, depriving the Invid of the Fruits needed for the mecha nutrient baths. And Tesla was still unaccounted for—although at times the Regent thought he could actually *feel* the traitor's bloodlusts reaching out for him.

Much the way he felt at the moment. Even his pets seemed stricken by the same lassitude. He overcame his mood somewhat when a servant entered to announce that an important message had been received. But it was the lieutenant's words that brought the Regent back to life.

"The Sentinels! Here?"

"Yes, m'lord. They are requesting permission to land. Four of their number are in need of treatments apparently only Haydon IV can provide. They are seeking a truce by way of surrender."

The Regent shot to his feet. "This is a dream!"

"No, m'lord."

The Regent stood motionless for a moment, then laughed. "Here! Of course they would surrender here, where to fire first means certain death." He reached up to feel his swollen cowl. "However..."

The lieutenant waited while the Regent paced in front of his throne. "Yes, yes, it could work." He swung around. "Inform the Sentinels that we accept their terms. And bring the Zor-clone to my chambers. I will put it to him simply: the matrix for the lives of his comrades. What could be more just?"

"May the Great Shaper Haydon watch over you this day," Teal told the the shuttle group from the balcony in the SDF-7's launch bay.

Vince, Cabell, Max, and the others saluted their friends as the hatch sealed itself. In a moment the shuttle's attitude jets flared, and the craft began to descend toward the green and silver crescent that was Haydon IV.

The second group numbered twelve, including the three Invid—one in each of the three armored Alpha Veritechs. Jack had a no-nonsense air about him as he strapped into the forward cockpit of his mecha. Bela was behind him; Gnea, Kami, and one of the scientists in the Beta module. Janice was piloting the second VT, with Burak in the copilot's seat, and Lron and Tesla in the Beta. The third VT held Learna, Crysta, and the second scientist. Jack had taken one last look at Rick, Lisa, and Karen before they had been moved into the shuttle, and the sight of their slack, colorless faces was with him now as he engaged the Alpha's thrusters and maneuvered the ship out of the launch bay. The SDF-7's human and XT crew had been instructed to keep the fortress clear of the Invid fleet, but in close enough proximity to Haydon IV's surface to eliminate any threat of an enemy sneak attack.

Veidt and Sarna had done their best to convince the Sentinels to abandon their plans for an unannounced approach, but Jack and the rest were determined to give it a try. Besides, it wasn't like they were going in with weapons blazing. Their approach would be a gentle one, Jack had insisted; a simple landing in the forests west of the planet's principal city. Surely, three small mecha weren't going to touch off Haydon IV's legendary (and somewhat questionable) defenses.

It is merely *intent*, Veidt had tried to tell them.

Jack heard the words surfacing in his thoughts, and made an effort to push them from his mind. In a moment he would be able to discern details of the planet's surface topography. It was bound to be an extraordinary sight—an entire world reconfigured to conform to the demands of its inhabitants.

Jack found himself wondering about the guiding intelligence behind such a feat.

Then he began to notice that the forest they had chosen as landing zone, was, well, *moving*—sliding east to west across the variegated landscape like some sort of by-pass door. And something very bizarre was rising up at them from the space that forest had vacated . . . Swirling vortices of energy, radiant silken scarves riding Haydon IV's savage updrafts.

Jack sent a telephathic plea to the planet: We've come in peace. *We've come in peace!*

The following chapter is a sneak preview of WORLD KILLERS—Book IV in the continuing saga of THE SENTINELS!!

CHAPTER
ONE

They were the New Paladins, riding forth to answer the trumpet call to a nightmare war.
They were mortals caught up in events that transcended anything they had ever expected.
Many of them were career military people who had learned that wars were often won by those who made the fewest screw-ups.
But they also knew that everybody screws up sometime.

Le Roy la Paz, *The Sentinels*

"**E**VERYBODY STAY SHARP! LOOKS LIKE WE'RE gonna haveta go to guns!"

Jack Baker trimmed the mated Veritechs he was flying —the sleek Alpha fighter now joined like a vaned nose cone to the bigger, burlier Beta ship. A quick glance over his weapons status displays revealed that the other two Alpha-Betas of his raiding party were still in tight formation behind him.

"Jack, *no!*" yelled Janice Em. She was in the second ship along with Burak, Lron, and Tesla. "You *heard* what Veidt and Sarna said. This world's defenses will respond to *any* hostile action!"

Actually, Veidt had said the legendery protective systems of the planet responded to the mere *intent* of intrusion or provocative act. And that certainly seemed to be the case today, even though the fighters had gone in with weapons and shields down.

"I got a news flash for you: we've *already* got Haydon IV PO'd at us, kiddo," Jack snorted. "Or d'you think this planet's surface *usually* twitches and then starts spitting sparklers at people? Get ready; like it or not, it looks as if we're in for some turns 'n burns."

One part of him registered the fact that the terrain of Haydon IV wasn't actually twitching; it was *changing shape*, like something from one of those oldtime clay animation flicks. And the things shooting up at the incoming Veritechs were more like swirling vortices or sheets of flame than sparklers.

Whatever they were, they were traveling at such a high velocity that Jack saw the VTs had no chance of running for it.

"Activate shields and weapons." Jack tried to sound calm. "And stay close to me." It was too late to go back, so there was nothing to do but *drive on*.

He only wished there were experienced combat fliers in the other two combined VTs. Jan had been through training, and so had Learna, but neither of them had any dogfighting experience to speak of. He would have preferred to have Max and Miriya Sterling flying at his wingtips.

But Miriya had been stricken, like Rick Hunter and his wife Lisa, by the strange microorganisms of Garuda. And so had another Sentinel, one whose possible death filled Jack with feelings and impulses that bewildered and shocked him . . .

He tried to put that out of his mind; what was happening to the famous Baker cool and concentration? *Damn!*

From the cockpit's rear seat, where she was strapped into the co-pilot's station, Bela reached forward to clap him on the shoulder. "That's the lad! Kick their flaming arses! I'll loan you the boot!"

The vortices of fire came darting and circling, changing shape and roiling—like silken scarves on the wind. All Jack's sensors were in alarm mode, but none of them could tell him what he was facing.

Fire with fire, he told himself fatalistically, and put a

burst of pumped-laser into the first one to come into range.

Somehow Tesla got on the tac net. "No, you *fool*! You're signing our death warrants!"

"Don't bother me; I'm workin'," Jack growled.

The cannonfire seemed to have no effect; the vortice changed course a bit and headed straight for him. He shot at it again. The other VTs chose targets of opportunity and opened up too.

The vortices flared angrily, and some were jarred, but they kept coming. More came from what seemed to be an opening in the countryside below, like flecks of incandescent paint flying upward.

Jack was still firing when the first vortice hit him. It flared angrily against his sheilds, sending the indicators toward the danger zones, and it seemed he could feel the infernal heat right through the fuselage. More swarmed after.

The other VTs were struck too. The vortices spread across them, coating them in a blinding radiance.

"Wake up! Come, come; I have no time for this nonsense! Wake him!"

Rem heard the thick, moist, rumbling voice, loud enough to echo and shake the walls. He associated it with the sensation he felt, now: bonds still holding his raw, bleeding wrists and ankles, and the cottony blur the Invid psy-scanners had left in his brain.

At the Regent's command, Invid Officers applied brief pain to speed the effects the reviving injections they had given him. Rem squirmed and moaned, shaking off part of the fog, and opened his eyes.

Rem saw the throneroom that the Regent had decreed for himself high in a Haydon IV Tower. It was a minor mercy to see the light of Briz'dziki, the local sun, rather than the cold insides of the Invid's nearby Hive.

Rem tried to recall what he was doing there, and it came back in a confused, horrifying rush. Capture by the Invid on Garuda; exposure to Garudan atmosphere—why wasn't he dead, or mad?

Or, perhaps he was—perhaps he was both.

No, he wasn't dead; the pain of his shackles was a branding-hot clarity too sharp for that. But mad . . .

As he struggled feebly, he heard a low, mosquitolike humming that quickly built until it shockwaved from one side of his skull to the other. The shackles seemed to grow teeth and gnaw at his wrists, promising to devour their way up his arms and legs, ripping and savaging.

Rem screamed. The Invid stench coagulated with evil glee in his chest—he was sure he would suffocate.

Not mad—but even more terribly, a victim of *hin*, the Garudan altered-reality or transcendent state.

Kami and Learna and their people thrived that way—in *hin*—as a matter of symbiotic course, in interaction with their environment on a microorganic, even sub-atomic scale. Stranded from the synergistic biota of their planet, they would not even be sentient beings.

But to outside lifeforms, exposure to the atmosphere of Garuda and to *hin* was a death sentence by insanity.

Rem fought to hold onto some last shred of reality. The seemingly endless memories of the Optera before his time, and the paradise it had been—had he only dreamed them? Images of the Regent's estranged mate, the Regis, and her passion for Zor, whose biogenetic material had been made manifest in Rem's cloning—were they too fever dreams of the *hin*? But they had seemed so real, not hallucinatory; more ordered and in focus than any dream or nightmare.

The Invid officers hoisted Rem to his feet with a clanking of his chains. To Rem's addled and tormented senses, the cold tiles felt like white-green frost, that burned the soles of his feet and froze them at the same time.

The Regent loomed before him, twenty feet high, massive and terrible, his mantle spread like a cobra's hood as he gazed down through liquid black eyes as big as manhole covers. Rem felt the *hin* seize him again, making the breath in his lungs coagulate and refuse to move.

Rem heard his own whimpering, felt his self control about to slip from his grasp. He had the abrupt impression that there were things in the shadows waiting to pounce upon him and feast on his marrow, then take his mind and steal his soul. And though a remote part of his intellect could recognize it as the mind-wrenching effect of *hin*, he couldn't find the strength or the will to fight it.

"Stand him up straight," the Regent said, when Rem would have pulled himself into a weeping fetal ball. "Hold his head up."

When Rem was standing up and staring wild-eyed as an animal with its leg in a trap, the Regent went on. "You're a very difficult fellow, Tiresian. Or should I say, 'Clone'? Or better yet, 'Zor-clone'?"

He held up four-fingered fists with wrists several times thicker than Rem's waist. "Whatever you *really* are, here's something that might interest you. Your Sentinel friends are coming."

Rem couldn't hide a wretched whimper of disbelief and despair mixed with crazed hope. The Regent caught it. "That's right: they are coming directly into my hands. To be imprisoned like you, to be put to the Inquisition like you, and to go through all the pain and mind-probing you've gone through."

Rem was nearly in tears, but the Regent was leaning forward in the colossal throne, drowning him out. "But it needn't happen that way! You can save them, Zor-clone, and save yourself as well! The Haydon IV healers can cure them and cure you too, this very hour; you can leave with them—if you'll simply say a few paltry words and give me what I want."

But Rem *was* broken. Courage and conviction and strength and faith—and even love—are overrated when it comes to defense against torture. Yet the Regent failed to incorporate one thing into his equations—the one factor that no agony could overcome: ignorance.

"Tell me where the last Protoculture matrix is," the Regent hissed. "Tell me where the original Zor sent it—hid it! You have many of his memories—how, I'm not sure. But that one *must* be there, it *must!*"

But it wasn't. If it had been, Rem would have yielded it up in a moment. That escape was closed to him, though.

Rem laid his head to his chest and sobbed. Deep in the *hin*, he felt the sunlight jeering at him, his fear-sweat turning to acid against his skin, panic closing off his windpipe.

He heard the creak as the Regent rose from his chair. "Above all things, I despise stubbornness. That, I punish."

Lynn-Minmei tried to stop the passageway from spinning as she lurched along, her hand held by the mysterious VT pilot; she was barefoot and disheveled, sick with the drinks she had downed but sicker still with her latest and worst glimpse of human nature.

Not that she had intentionally drank a lot; she had nothing but contempt for drunkards. But life as the consort of general T. R. Edwards was a little easier to bear after a round or two. And then there was the drink itself—from Edwards's private bottle—something she had heard the top-eschelon officers jokingly call "weed-whacker."

It was a 150-proof vacuum distillate that had been soaked in fibers from a plant related to the Flower of Life, and strained out again. Brackish; deadly. But oddly smooth and warming.

Best taken by the slow shot glass.

But, she had needed *something* to fortify her as she sat there and listened to Edwards—the man Minmei had thought she loved, the man to whom she had given herself—reveal himself as a devil incarnate.

She was dizzy, and thought she might lose her balance, or her lunch—she had had no dinner. "Wait, wait," she puffed, breathless. Her head spun, and she tasted bile in the back of her throat.

The VT pilot stopped and turned to her, gesturing in a way that made it clear he was concerned about her. Minmei brushed her hair out of her eyes yet again, to study him. "Do I know you? Who *are* you?"

He was tall and lean, and demonstrated a supple

strength. Behind the tinted facebowl of his flight helmet, all she could discern was the dark, thick beard. He regarded her for a moment, then answered, "It says right here: REF Service #666-60-937."

She could *see* that, and his flight officer's insignia and unit flash. But his name tape, stitched over his left breast pocket, was unfamiliar: *Isle, L.* His voice, coming through the helmet's tinny external speaker, was unrecognizable.

Her mystery savior was wearing the unit patch of one of the outfits from Dr. Lang's research facility. Lang had managed to ram through the council an authorization for his *own* security forces, but Edwards had fought the seconding of pilots to the Robotech scientist. So, this was almost certainly one of the fliers who had been selected from the lower ranks and trained on Tirol to fill the cockpits of Lang's personal army.

But what was he doing on SDF-3?

Minmei swayed slowly from side to side, closing one eye in an effort to focus on him. "C'mon, c'mon; I mean, why're y'*doing* this?" She still wasn't sure he wouldn't drag her back to Edwards—maybe to claim some kind of reward or favor.

She was also waiting for the alarms to go off.

Surely by now Edwards had realized that she hadn't simply fled his embrace and his bedroom for some fresh air. Even vain, cold Edwards must have admitted to himself by now that Minmei had made a break for freedom.

"You said you want to go to Tiresia, didn't you?" the VT flier was saying. "And perhaps to Garuda, or Haydon IV? I'll see that you get to wherever you want to go, Minmei. But Tiresia's the obligatory first stop."

There was some resonance in his voice, even over the speaker, that she thought she recognized. Minmei sighed and ran her hand through her fine black hair again. Plainly, no VT could make a star-jump; and the few remaining REF vessels that could go superluminal were scarcely the kind of spacecraft you could sign out like a borrowed fanjet.

But there was something in the man's tone, something

steely and yet compassionate, that didn't sound like it brooked failure.

She vaguely remembered saying to him, outside Edwards's quarters, that she wanted to go to Tiresia or Garuda, but the beginning of their adventure was lost in an alchoholic mini-blackout. She was not sure what her plan had been, though, except that Jonathan Wolff and Rick Hunter were out there someplace.

She shook her head slowly, "I don't—I don't . . ."

He took her hand again. "Don't worry, Minmei."

Then he led her off again. Minmei lost track of things for a while, but blearily realized at one point that he was shoving oversize deck slippers onto her bare feet. At another point, she felt something sting her arm and saw that he had given her a shot with a medikit ampule.

"Anti-nausea," REF #666-60-937 explained. "It makes it tough to see out the cockpit canopy if you heave your cookies."

"'Cockpit'?" she repeated, trying to figure out what he was getting at. Then she realized that he had her standing near a hatch that led to a hangar deck. There were the distant whines of VTs being readied for flight.

"Wait right here," he said after he led her into the vast, mostly darkened hangar deck. Minmei did not get to ask what he was doing; he was gone.

The anti-nausea drug settled her queasiness and brought her around a bit too. She was drawing deep breaths and burping a bit, sitting on the deck, when he caught her hands and pulled Minmei upward.

"All set; just follow me. That's our ship over there."

"Wh—"

And then they were walking among the parked mecha of the hangar deck. Welding sparks and humming maint-crew machinery made noise in the distance, and she could hear men and women yelling or cursing or cajoling or laughing as they sweated to keep the REF's fighting forces operational.

He was leading her toward an armored Alpha, a lusterless gray fighter trimmed in olive drab, bulked by its augmentation pods. It was one of the most formidable ships in the REF inventory, and she didn't think it possible that it had been assigned to one of Lang's "six-month-wonder" pilots.

Minmei saw the boarding ladder before her and it brought back a flood of memories. She was a non-tech person; why did mecha insist on playing such an overwhelming part in her life?

Then somebody yelled from the distance, and more voices took up the cry. She realized woozily that the voices were coming her way. She had both hands on the boarding ladder and one foot on the first rung when she became aware of a ruckus behind her.

By the time she turned around, there were three or four flight deck personnel laid out flat, unconscious. Minmei blinked at them owlishly. *What—*

Then REF #666-60-937 was pushing her up the ladder, loading her into the copilot's seat and then belting her in. Apparently he knew all the right codes; the launch cat airlock accepted the powerful Alpha fighter and flung it out into space.

Green, looming Fantoma cast its light on them and their ship, and Tirol was a gibbous splotch of orange-brown-gray not far from it. The VT pilot turned his craft toward Tirol.

Suddenly his instruments were squealing and beeping for his attention. "Hot scramble from SDF-3, of course," she heard him mutter. "They want you back. They're coming to get you."

"Then—"

"Sit tight." He hit the auxiliaries for full military power and dove toward Tirol. Eager pursuers formed up for the hunt.

Minmei, pressed back in her seat, looking out at the unknowable stars, felt tears pressed from her eyes by acceleration, to wet the headrest behind her.

"Here they come," said REF #666-60-937.

ABOUT THE AUTHOR

Jack McKinney has been a psychiatric aide, fusion-rock guitarist and session man, worldwide wilderness guide, and "consultant" to the U.S. Military in Southeast Asia (although they had to draft him for that).

His numerous other works of mainstream and science fiction—novels, radio and television scripts—have been written under various pseudonyms.

He currently resides in Ubud, on the Indonesian island of Bali.